T0129871

The Legend of Corky Sandoval

PHIL PERKINS

authorHOUSE®

AuthorHouse™
1663 Liberty Drive
Bloomington, IN 47403
www.authorhouse.com
Phone: 1 (800) 839-8640

Published by AuthorHouse 10/26/2018

ISBN: 978-1-5462-6562-7 (sc)
ISBN: 978-1-5462-6563-4 (e)

Library of Congress Control Number: 2018912787

Print information available on the last page.

Any people depicted in stock imagery provided by Getty Images are models,
and such images are being used for illustrative purposes only.
Certain stock imagery © Getty Images.

This book is printed on acid-free paper.

Because of the dynamic nature of the Internet, any web addresses or
links contained in this book may have changed since publication and
may no longer be valid. The views expressed in this work are solely those
of the author and do not necessarily reflect the views of the publisher,
and the publisher hereby disclaims any responsibility for them.

Jacket Design by Sandra Dube
Copy Editor Bethany Halle
Cover Photo by Kaapo

Thank You

I would like to thank surfing legend Corky Carroll for helping me keep it real. His encouragement and knowledge of this great sport made the writing of this book even more enjoyable and rewarding.

Phil

Additional story ideas and semi-true
recollections by Sandra Dube

Expert coaching and background color by Bethany Halle

Even more surf cred by Mike Weisenberger

Contents

Prologue

"It's a semi-true story
Believe it or not
I made up a few things
And there's some I forgot
But the life and the telling
Are both real to me
And they all run together
And turn out to be, a semi-true story"

Written by Mac McAnally
Performed by Jimmy Buffett

Chapter One

THE LEGEND BEGINS

It was 1966. The World Surfing Championship, Ocean Beach, San Diego, California. Surf was up. No, I mean literally the surf was UP. Let me put you in that moment. We were all waiting for the judges to indicate that the competition could begin. It had been a long haul getting to that point. Our beloved sport had been viewed as nothing more than a childish leisure pursuit by mostly lazy beach bums. But we knew better. True believers knew that surfing would become a worldwide phenomenon and respected competitive sport.

Well, maybe not but we had crystal clear delusions of grandeur.

I must admit to being intimidated by the talent assembled for what was my first really big surfing competition. I recognized the names of most of the competitors of course. But all of a sudden, I'm standing within sand kicking distance of Nat Young and David Nuuhiwa. There were some big reputations waiting on that beach. I was aware that David was renowned for being a nose rider. They say he could perch on the tip of the board for up to twenty seconds. That was definitely not my forte. Instant wipeout.

Some of the best surfers could surf both regular and goofy foot. I promised myself I wouldn't bog you down with unfamiliar surf lingo, so for the uninitiated a 'goofy foot' surfs with his or her right foot forward. If you watch surfers at the beach, you will notice that most surfers surf with their left foot out front. While they may walk the board on occasion they usually come back to that stance.

For no particular reason you may be interested to know that I'm a goofy foot.

My name is Corky Sandoval. I've been surfing for a good while, but I must admit that this was my first real test, a real competition. I didn't have high expectations, but in that situation and with unpredictable surf you never know.

A little background. I was born in Laguna Beach, California but we moved to Oahu during my high school years. My dad, Bob Sandoval, was stationed there with the Navy. You might think from my last name that I'm Hispanic. But I never heard of any Spanish in my background except from one looney uncle who said we were descended from Diego De Sandoval, a Spanish explorer and conquistador in the 1500s. Who knows, maybe Uncle Dan was right.

You might also wonder how I got my nickname. Well my dad had the idea that the best way to teach me to swim was just to throw me in the pool a few times. Turns out I always popped right back to the top. So, he started to call me 'Corktop'. After a while that just evolved into Corky.

All of the kids that I went to school with on Oahu surfed. Surfing is to kids in Hawaii as little league is to haoles from the mainland. Oh sorry, a haole is basically a non-Hawaiian. I won't go into any more detail on that but let's just say I was one but at the time didn't really want to be. I wanted to be a Native Hawaiian or maoli more than anything in the world. Oh well. At least I learned to surf.

And then there were the girls. If you didn't surf you didn't exist. I mean even the girls surfed. If you sat and watched…well, from a scoring standpoint, you sat and watched. Might as well have had your nose in a book (not that there's anything really wrong with that. After all, you may have your nose in a book right now. Sorry 'bout that). I quickly realized that dating and surfing went hand in hand and without the ability to ride the waves, you just wouldn't go hand in hand with any girl on the island. Or maybe it just seemed that way to a haole.

After a while, I got good enough at surfing to enter some local competitions. I even won a small event on Maui but generally wasn't 'in the money'. Not that there was much money at stake in those days. I mean, you often got a trophy or a gift certificate or something along those lines, but no-one made a living at surfing, at least not in my neighborhood.

But I kept plugging away at it and once I graduated from high school and started thinking about college or a life of leisure, I was pretty darned good at the sport I loved. I quickly decided to take a couple of years off and just surf the world. Heck, college would still be there when I had had my fill of surfing.

So, I returned to Cali and began surfing in competitions up and down the coast. Now, I know you envision me driving the Pacific Coast Highway in my 'woodie', blond hair flying in the salty ocean breeze with surfer girl by my side, but that couldn't be further from the real experience. First of all, I'm not a blond. I have dark brown hair. I tried bleaching my hair once and it turned out orange. Experiment in 'cool' officially over.

As for the woodie, not so much. What I did have was an old Plymouth my dad gave me. Still, out of necessity I did mount my board on the top of the vehicle and named it 'the Buggy'. Maybe that satisfies your mental image somewhat.

And that surfer girl? Nope. Mostly I traveled with my buddy Kaapo from high school. Kaapo was a real Hawaiian, a real maoli, and that was his given name in Hawaiian culture. He told me that it's actually a Finnish version of Gabriel, so he insisted I called him Gabe. Whatever.

Now except for my name, which a lot of people said made me at least *sound* like a surfer, I guess I didn't really fit the mold of the surfer community in those days, although one girl I dated for a while insisted on calling me Moondoggy. Oh well.

So here we were in San Diego and the Ocean Beach competition. I knew I was outclassed but I'm just bullheaded enough to have thought I would have a chance of at least placing.

As you might expect, I didn't do very well in that big competition. As predicted, Nat Young won with his revolutionary new board 'Magic Sam'. But I wasn't discouraged. In fact, I grew more committed.

And now at least I'd competed in a major event. I was clearly outclassed, but I still felt with some practice I could up my game and be competitive in some of the tournaments around the West Coast.

After nearly a year of bumming around Southern California, surfing small competitions and waiting tables, Gabe convinced me to move on and head up towards the San Francisco area to a little place called Half Moon Bay. Later it would become the home of the famous Mavericks big wave event but at that point it was just a sleepy little town. It's about thirty-five miles south of San Francisco and has lots of interesting history and a routinely ridable surf. I got a kick out of hearing about the rumrunners, who during Prohibition used the hidden coves and fog cover to allow them to move their goods into the Bay area undetected. So off we went.

We got into town one Tuesday about lunch time and found a diner called Bennie's not far from the beach. The entire place (which wasn't much more than a greasy spoon) was done up in surf memorabilia. As we sat down at our table, I looked around at the pictures on the wall. They were of local stars of the waves and their longboards smiling as if they had just scored a major win. All were in stark black and white.

An older man, who appeared to run the place, along with one waitress, were there along with a few people picking away at burgers and fries but otherwise the place was pretty desolate. The waitress headed for our table right away.

"Hi, my name is Abby and I'll be taking your order. Our special today is a North Carolina style barbeque with slaw and fries. Any interest?"

"Wow, that sounds pretty good to me," I said, while thinking a whole lot less about lunch and much more about this beautiful girl.

Abby was in her late teens or early twenties with long red hair and a spray of freckles on each cheek. I noticed right away that her eyes were a bright blue, almost the color of the Pacific Ocean on a sunny day. When she spoke, her voice was breathy and to a young guy with stars in his eyes, pretty sexy. She was dressed in a peasant blouse and long skirt and looked to me like the hippie pictures I saw from stories about San Francisco. I noticed right away that she was barefoot, which seemed pretty strange in a restaurant. But that was just her way and it didn't seem to faze the old man.

With mouth watering (…tsk tsk…I mean about the food) I ordered the special while Gabe ordered a Taco plate.

"Ya got to stay in shape, Corky. Lay off the big ass sandwiches will ya?"

"Ah come on, Gabe, let a guy have a little fun. Anyway, Tacos aren't much better."

As we had traveled up the PCH, Gabe had convinced me that he could find a way to make us both money from my decent but relatively rudimental surfing skills.

"From now on, I'm your manager," he said, smiling broadly. You see the irony is that, regardless of what I told you about the girls, Kaapo (…ummmm. Gabe) was practically the only Hawaiian I knew that didn't surf. But he had the gift of gab (or as he called it 'the gift of Gabe') and impressed the girls with his wit and presumed wisdom, even as he bummed around the beach and did pretty much nothing.

So, he proposed to use the 'gift of Gabe' to promote me into some competitions where I actually had a chance of winning. Mostly those with no big names like Nat Young or Corky Carroll anywhere to be found. I should note that of all the champion class surfers in those days, Corky Carroll was my idol. You have to believe me when I say my nickname was just a coincidence. No really, I promise. When it finally dawned on me that I had the same nickname as one of the real stars, I guess I just rationalized that Corky wouldn't mind, so I went with it. I grew up Corky, might as well surf as Corky. Turns out the 'coincidence' would serve me well as time went on, but more on that later.

Abby soon brought us our orders and since the place wasn't busy, we convinced her to sit down with us a while.

"Where are you guys from?"

"A little bit of everywhere," Gabe said, taking the lead. "Wherever the surf's up…Hawaii, Orange County. You name it, my boy has surfed it," he continued in this lilting island accent.

"Oh, should I have heard of you?" Abby asked, looking at me.

Somehow, I knew this girl wasn't an expert in surfing, or at least not someone who followed the sport routinely.

"Maybe so. My name is Corky Sandoval and not too long ago I crushed the World Championship in San Diego."

I have no idea why I answered with what in reality was a giant lie but impressing her seemed at the time to be the most important thing in the world. Gabe's eyes got really big as soon as the sentence left my lips, of course.

"Wow! How did you end up here? I thought the big surf was further south," she asked.

"We're just tooling up the PCH and seeing where it takes us," I responded. "I'll do some surfing along the way, but we mainly just want to see California before heading to college or whatever."

"What about the draft?" she asked, as lots of people did in those days.

"Gabe and I are physically unfit to serve," using the wording I once heard used for 4F. Mine had to do with a heart condition. It didn't bother me otherwise, but I wasn't about to argue.

"Ah, come on Corky. Why do you always have to say it that way?" Gabe looked genuinely annoyed.

"You guys don't look much like surfers, too clean cut or something."

"Well, we're working on it," Gabe offered up.

At that time, Gabe looked fairly native with a bit of Japanese thrown in for good measure. Sort of like a younger Don Ho. He was in shape because of being on the wrestling team but was too, how can I say this, 'chunky' to look much like a surfer. With only a few exceptions, surfers tended to be fairly thin and some pretty tall. I don't think there was a perfect build to become competitive but being a bit wiry didn't hurt.

I was working on growing my hair out some, but I wasn't very far along, so I probably still looked the college prep kid that I actually had been. But like Gabe said, we were working on it.

"So, are you guys planning on staying around for a day or so?" Abby asked.

"Depends on the surf and what there is to do around here," I responded.

We went on with our lunch and Abby swung by our table to check on us a time or two. Soon it was time to pay the check and I called her over.

"Abby, we don't know the area very well. Would you be able to show us around after you get off and maybe have a drink with us?"

You could tell the waitress hesitated to accept since she didn't know these out-of-towners, but she must have figured we were 'safe as milk' as the saying goes.

"Sure, I can show you around. If you drop by here around four, we can drive around and see the sights. Not much to see really but a great view of the ocean.'

"Maybe we can even buy you dinner," I ventured, even though I knew funds were short.

"That's not necessary but I accept," she said with a little chuckle.

"See you then," Gabe told her.

At four o'clock, we returned to the diner and the three of us headed out on our little excursion. Abby was a skilled guide and pointed out only the finest grubby bars and burger joints. Guess she knew those would end up being our home away from home for a few days.

With our funds severely limited, we managed to find a little eatery that served several different types of meals from Mexican to Italian. We found out pretty quickly that Abby didn't eat meat, so she spent some time trying to piece together a dinner she could enjoy. Meanwhile, I think Gabe was secretly counting our cash and glancing at the menu to try to cause us as little embarrassment as possible.

Luckily, we were able cover the tab, including one beer each and still have a few bucks for breakfast.

To satisfy a young man's need for sleep, we carried a tent in the Buggy that was pretty easy to pitch on the beach. To get there we had to actually hike down a steep trail to reach to the water's edge. The famous "cliffs" along the ocean front loomed above us. As the sun set we found a good spot in a rocky area back from the tidepools a bit. We'd had researched the tides and used dead reckoning to ensure we wouldn't wake up under water. An early dinner made it possible for us to get to the beach in time to watch the sunset. And what a sunset it was. I don't think I'd ever seen that mix of orange, yellow and red like that. The whole display was even more amazing reflected in the active ocean. The scene took my breath away.

Unfortunately, our tour with Abby had ruled out surfing that day. But tomorrow was another day.

As we sat there that evening, watching the waves roll in and listening to the crashing surf, I made an important decision. The ocean would be my playground for as long as I enjoyed the challenge of the surf. I wanted to improve enough to be a part of the elite group of Nat, David and the other for real Corky. Tall order. But I was young and determined.

That was the end of a beautiful day.

Chapter Two

THE HALF MOON WAY

The next morning Gabe woke before I did and was down by the water, presumably trying to catch our breakfast. Didn't look as though he was having much luck. Later we found out that surf fishing wasn't something that Half Moon Bay was famous for. Anyway, Gabe didn't really know what he was doing in the fishing department.

We had a small coffee pot and were able to build a little fire and get the day started with a very strong cup of Kona. Maybe it was the sparkling morning, or the mix of the salty sea air, but I don't think coffee ever smelled that good to me. It smelled like the first morning of the rest of my life. Pretty soon the conversation turned to how we would spend that day and for that matter the next few weeks.

"You know, Gabe, I think I'd like to hang around here for a while."

"Is it the girl, Corky? Cause if so, I don't want to be the third wheel."

"No, not really. She's cute and all. but it's really just the vibe here. I think I'd like to try to earn a few bucks before we move on anyway. You up for it?"

"Sure, whatever you think. I've got time on my hands," Gabe chuckled. "But what kind of gig are you thinking about finding?"

"I was thinking about seeing if the old man at the diner needed any extra help and might be able to throw me a shift or two."

"Cool. I'll look around too and see what I might be able to find that's not too much work but still legal…or at least mostly.", Gabe said smiling that mischievous smile that was his trademark.

I decided to surf for a while that morning. Gabe made up his mind to do what he did best, lay on the beach and hatch plans. We could begin our job searches that afternoon. The ocean was a bit glassy that day, but I was able to catch a couple of pretty good waves before giving up.

Our breakfast ended up being some fruit from a street vendor, but that combined with nearly perfect weather really hit the spot and bolstered our spirits.

I found my way over to Bennie's to see if there was any possibility of work while Gabe took the Buggy and drove around looking for 'help wanted' signs. Good luck with that.

Abby was there when I arrived, and I filled her in on what I had in mind. I asked her if the old man was there and she corrected me instantly.

"If you have any hope of working here you'd better call him by his name, Ben or Mr. Colter. He's owned this place for twenty-five years and is pretty set in his ways, so be extra courteous."

Ah, now I knew where the name Bennie's came from.

Abby took me to the back of the diner where Mr. Colter was cleaning a grill.

"Mr. Colter, I'd like for you to meet Corky Sandoval, Corky, Mr. Colter," she said, introducing him with a lot of pride.

Mr. Colter was a man in at least his sixties. You could tell he had been pretty tall, but age had bent him over slightly. He had a full head of rumpled hair that was white as snow. His skin was weather-beaten and brown as a leather saddle.

"Hello son," he said in a voice testifying to the fact that he was or had been a smoker. "You can call me Ben."

He stuck out his gnarled hand to shake mine and nearly broke a finger or two.

"I think I saw you in here yesterday didn't I, Corky?", Ben said, looking at me as if trying to place my face.

"Yes sir, I had a great lunch. Couldn't have been better."

"Corky is a pretty well-known surfer in Southern California I guess," Abby offered.

"Well yes… I think I've heard your name before." Ben seemed genuinely impressed.

Here we go again! At that moment I wasn't motivated to correct him.

I've done a little surfing myself," Ben said. "Getting a little old for it now, but I still manage a small break once in a while."

"Be honest, Ben, in your day you were the best around here," Abby said, pointing to a large picture on the wall above the grill.

It was of a young buff looking guy riding what appeared to be a gigantic wave. He looked really comfortable on his longboard and was actually smiling in the picture.

"I mostly surfed around this neck of the woods," Ben said, "but did manage to do some traveling in the southern part of California. Don't let Abby fool you, though, I wasn't that good, just devoted." He laughed out loud.

"Come on, Ben, be real," Abby corrected. "Ben twice won the challenge put on by Franks Place." Franks Place was a famous eatery right on the ocean. It had a bit of a shady past, but we learned that it was an institution in Half Moon Bay.

"So, what can I do for you, Corky?" Ben asked.

"I was wondering if you needed an extra hand waiting tables at peak times."

Ben again laughed out loud. "I'm not sure we have any peak times do we Abby?" he joked.

"Well it gets a bit busy with the after-work crowd. Maybe we could use Corky a couple of nights a week during that part of the day."

Ben pondered the thought, rubbing his forehead as he did.

"Sure, I'll give you a try, Corky. Can't resist helping out a fellow surfer, particularly one with your reputation." I cringed again but stayed silent.

And so, it began. I served enough burgers and beer to keep myself and, for that matter Gabe, on the very same diet.

As time went on, I got to know Abby pretty well. Her background was pure 'white bread'. She was raised in nearby Alameda, California and her folks ran an inn. She was a high school achiever, graduating in the top five percent of her class. She was even a cheerleader but seemed embarrassed by that fact.

Once Abby graduated from high school, she almost immediately moved from her parent's home and headed for the bay. It wasn't 'til later that I found out why and that she had been here before. Clearly, Half Moon Bay offered up just the bohemian environment she was looking for, so like me, she decided to hang out for a while.

Meanwhile, Gabe had found a gig at a car wash of sorts and was making fairly good money, mostly from tips. So, we were able to rent a room in a small motel off the beach. We even had a hotplate for our coffee. Between working and surfing (or in Gabe's case loafing), life hit a very comfortable groove.

Abby and I flirted with that old boyfriend, girlfriend thing as you probably guessed, but both of us decided we were better off just being buddies. Well, it was mostly her decision, but you know what I mean.

One evening after being in Half Moon Bay for about a month and a half, the three of us were sitting on the beach waiting for the sunset when it occurred to me to ask Abby a question.

"So, what's next for you?"

Abby looked like she was in deep thought before answering.

"I think I want to just travel for a while. I hate the idea of hitchhiking but that might have to be my ride.", she replied never taking her eyes off of the ocean and crashing waves.

"Where do you plan on heading?" Gabe asked.

"I want to start working my way east," Abby answered. "I've seen a lot of California but not much of the rest of the country. The furthest east I've been is Las Vegas. We have family there of all places."

"I guess I've thought of doing that same thing. Maybe we could just stick together and see the country. Beats hitchhiking," I ventured.

"Hey, Corkman," Gabe spoke up. "Not much surf in Idaho. Just sayin'."

"True, but there are some bitchin potatoes I'm told."

We all chuckled.

"But seriously, Gabe, I'm like Abby. I want to see more of the country. Maybe we can end up on the east coast eventually."

"Do they actually surf over there, Corky?" Gabe asked rolling his eyes.

"Well I've heard there is some sort of East Coast championship somewhere in the mid-Atlantic, Virginia, North Carolina. Dunno, but there must be some surf."

"Do they surf on the great lakes?" Abby asked earnestly, finally turning her attention back to her companions.

Both Gabe and I laughed but in fact we had no idea. Might be worth finding out one day I guess.

We sat there for a long while that evening, mostly in silence, just taking in the raw beauty of the ocean and the sound of the gulls. Abby again seemed mesmerized.

We didn't talk any more about making travel plans for several days, mainly because if all three of us pooled our money we'd have about a hundred bucks…maybe a hundred and a half. That would mean we'd need to find work almost immediately and the prospect of working some nothing job in Utah didn't ring any chimes for any of us.

Luckily business had actually picked up at Bennies and both Abby and I were making some pretty good tips. For the life of me I couldn't understand where the happy hour crowd came from. There was no real industry in Half Moon Bay. I soon learned many were college kids from across the bay who wanted to at least *see* the big waves if not put a board in the water. In addition, we drew the local restaurant and tourism workers.

Over time I got to know a couple of the regulars well enough to ask for advice about our travels east. One guy was from Wisconsin and he confirmed that people really did surf on Lake Michigan. Huh? I had no clue. But then at that point I often had no clue.

So, I made a note to try to swing by that Midwest state sometime in the future to see for myself. Of course, Gabe was dumbfounded.

"You want to go where? Wisconsin? What are you a cheese freak?" Gabe asked.

I explained to Gabe what I learned about the surf on the 'big lake' and he finally understood the pull, even if I wasn't absolutely sure. But we put Milwaukee on our growing list of places to visit. It was a good while before we could convince ourselves to go that far north though.

Another of the regular customers was a guy named Jessie. He was around nineteen and came in about twice a week with a little muttly terrier called Skipper. Skipper was a mix of breeds, but his brindle coat meant he was likely part Boston Terrier. At least that's what Jessie told us.

Officially the city of Half Moon Bay frowned on dogs inside eating establishments, but clearly Ben fell in love with the little guy and anyway, couldn't have cared less about what the city leaders liked or didn't like.

In talking with Jessie, I learned that he'd been drafted and was preparing for military service. While he didn't look forward to the gig he seemed resigned. He did tell me that he was working pretty hard to find someone to take Skipper in. He'd asked Ben and while the old man considered it, he told Jessie his routine wouldn't allow time to take care of the pooch.

After a fairly lengthy and spirited discussion with my partners in crime and eastward travelers, we decided to adopt Skipper. Oh brother, just what we needed, another mouth to feed. But the little mutt was just too damn cute to leave behind.

We did ask Jessie how Skipper got his name. Jessie said he adopted Skipper after a merchant marine captain died and his family just couldn't handle the little guy. So, Jessie named him, or maybe renamed him, Skipper in honor of the old sea captain. We all thought that as cool as tap water.

After another week or so Jessie came in to say goodbye. He was on his way to training camp and in full uniform. His hair was freshly cropped and he looked every bit the soldier. I could tell by his face that he was scared, but then our whole generation grew up scared. I did my best to perk him up, mostly by giving him a couple of beers on the house. That seemed to mellow him out a bit. After we talked some more he headed out. At that moment we didn't know if we would ever see him again.

But we did have Skipper and he was a constant source of humorous behavior and full of mischief. We tried to involve him in some human stuff. I even got him up on a board and he rode the small wave about twenty feet before going in head first. After shaking himself like dogs do, he looked at me like *come on, Corky. Jeez.*

One evening Gabe, Abby and I were walking along the beach and making plans when Gabe pointed out that if we were going to actually do this thing, we needed to travel the first mile. It did seem like we were dragging our feet, but the pull of the ocean was strong, and the bay area was heaven on earth. None-the-less, we decided it was time to firm up our plans.

Of course, part of the preparations involved telling Ben. Neither Abby nor I looked forward to that. Ben had been very good to both of us. We owed him a little notice and vowed to hang around for at least two more weeks while he found replacements. But we knew we had to let him know right away and decided to tell him after our shift on the following day.

Clearly Abby had to be the spokesman. After all, she'd known this cool old man for a good while and you could tell he doted on her.

We sat in a booth and Abby started to tell Ben about our decision but barely got out a word.

"Abby," Ben interrupted, "You can save your breath. I know you kids are leaving. It was only a matter of time. Hell, I'd do the same thing if I were your age. I don't want you to worry."

But Abby's eyes teared up and she began to apologize.

"Not necessary," assured Ben, an understanding almost fatherly look in his eyes.

That evening we got together for dinner and were all bummed. Abby had a good cry and Gabe and I sat wordlessly eating some godawful vegetarian meal Abby forced on us. Maybe that's the real reason she was crying.

Next day, Ben told Abby he wanted to talk with both of us. I must admit I worried that he had reconsidered his acceptance of our decision. Nothing could have been further from the truth.

Sitting in that same booth Ben said, "Since I can't go with you, I want to make a contribution to help you reach your goal and make your journey a little easier."

With that, Ben handed Abby a fist full of cash. Turned out to be a thousand dollars. I was totally shocked. Frankly, I wasn't used to that sort of kindness and understanding from the older generation, but Ben was a different sort of guy. He believed in chasing dreams and living life.

Abby teared up again and after many words of appreciation we both hugged the old man. I don't think I'll ever forget him. He became an inspiration later in my life, but that's a story yet to be told.

Several days later we headed out for the adventure of a lifetime. Surf's up again!

Chapter Three

ON SKIP AND THE STRIP

We had no real plan nor any idea where we would end up. But starting with Las Vegas seemed logical since Abby had family there. Two of her cousins had moved there a couple of years before and both worked at the spankin' new Caesar's Palace. We took turns driving and covered the nine-hour drive from Half Moon Bay in good order.

As you might guess, we hadn't given much thought to where we would stay once we arrived or how long we would be there. Finally, we located a small motel called LaConcha. Seemed clean enough and wasn't as expensive as the larger casino hotels. They weren't very busy, and we were actually able to negotiate getting two adjoining rooms for only a little more than one room.

Abby settled down in one room and Gabe and I threw our bags down in the other. Abby had taken to Skipper almost instantly and mothered him non-stop. Luckily when Jessie brought him to us, he had a little crate and assured us that Skipper was used to napping in it for short periods. So, after settling him in and throwing some water in our faces, we decided to set off for a little tour of this growing town.

Is seemed like there was new construction on every corner as we worked our way up what would become one of the most famous streets in America. There were neon signs everywhere and street hucksters tried to stop you on every corner to offer you everything from buffet tickets, to tours to strip shows. I think all of us were fascinated but a little surprised by the seediness of the place.

Abby suggested we head up to Caesar's to see if her cousins were working. Both were croupiers. She admitted that she had no idea how they learned the trade since gambling was then a really localized vice.

We walked into Caesar's and were immediately impressed with the flash and whizbang. It seemed more like Disney than a gambling palace. Looking around, we noticed that some gamblers seemed in almost a trance like state. Not being a gambler, I guess I didn't understand but Gabe couldn't take his eyes off the games.

Finally, he looked at us and said, "Do you think you guys could stake me for a while?"

"Stake you. What the heck does that mean?" I asked, lacking any knowledge of gambling jargon.

"You know, front me the money to do a little gambling. I know I can make us some extra bread for our travels."

Abby and I looked at each other, both of us clearly reluctant to give up even a little of the 'grub stake' Ben Colter had given us. But Gabe kept up with the persuasion and we finally agreed to front him a hundred dollars with the promise that was it. No more, no matter what. He seemed in another world as he headed off to pursue the winnings that we assumed were illusive in this town.

Unsure of where to start looking for Abby's cousins, or even if they were working that shift, we asked a waitress where to find the personnel department. Of course, she told us she didn't know if they were hiring, but we explained our predicament and she gave us the directions.

Turned out that Abby's cousins were both working tables that day and we headed off to seek them out. Her cousins were Jimmy Musgrave and his brother Sam. Both were in their mid-twenties I guessed and born and raised in middle America. It seemed like both could have been named Sven since the two brothers had long, blond locks and looked like they had spent the winter on the slopes. We knew we couldn't distract them from their gigs but wanted them to know we were in the building.

We found Sam first and after a quick chat he pointed to another table where Jimmy was working. We agreed to meet after their shift for a drink, which unfortunately was around eleven PM. We dropped by Jimmy's table, said hello and invited him to join us later. He readily agreed, seeming very happy to see his red headed cousin.

With that we walked around the brand-new casino and began trying to track Gabe down. We finally found him at a craps table and noticed he had a stack of chips, not a big one but it looked pretty impressive to us.

After some coaxing, we finally convinced him to cash out and come with us to dinner. We were both impressed to learn that he'd won just over three hundred dollars as promised. That improved our chances of a nutritious dinner considerably and we quickly located one of the restaurants inside the casino.

"Maybe we should stay here for a week or so," Gabe said. "I know I can double or triple our money."

"Not gonna happen, bro," I replied. "I have an idea your luck would run out and we really need to get back on the road soon."

"Anyway, Jack Benny is performing here. How cool is that?", he replied with that "star struck" look on his face.

Abby and I looked at each other and rolled our eyes.

"That alone would drive me out of town," I said.

Gabe looked disappointed, but I think he knew I was right about moving on. Well at least we were better off than when we arrived at the casino.

Later that evening, after hiking back to the motel to feed Skipper and take him for a walk, we met Jimmy and Sam for a drink in a little sideline bar area at Caesars. They were both nice enough even if they seemed a little cynical.

Abby was in the process of telling the cousins about California in general and Half Moon Bay more specifically when Jimmy piped up.

"So Corky, you're a surfer. Your name sounds kind of familiar. Should I have heard of you?"

"Nah.", I said, lowering my eyes to avoid Jimmy's.

Abby glanced at me, but I figured enough was enough.

"We only see surfing in movies I guess. What are you doing in Vegas? Ya can't surf in a swimming pool!", Jimmy continued with his questions.

I couldn't help but chuckle.

"Actually, just passing through, headed east", I explained, having another sip of my gin tonic.

"Is that what you call a surfin' safari?" Sam laughed.

"Only in a Beachboys song," Gabe chimed in.

"So how did you guys end up here?" I asked.

"I guess we just heard about what was happening in Las Vegas and it seemed like a great place to find a little night life, plus there's the showgirls. Sorry Abbs," Jimmy replied.

"No offense taken, cuz. I see what you mean.", Abby said, taking Jimmy off the hook.

"But like you guys, we'll likely move on maybe after a few months of padding the wallet a bit.", Jimmy continued.

"Where do you think you'll go next?" Gabe asked.

"Well our plan is to go in the opposite direction and end up somewhere on the west coast," Jimmy explained." In fact, maybe you can give us some advice."

"Sure," I replied without hesitation. "And here's my advice. Avoid LA at all costs".

"Hmmm... Why?" Sam questioned.

"The traffic is so bad that on a good day it can take you two hours to travel ten miles and it's getting worse all the time. If you end up in California, go either north or south of that city. Trust me."

I was giving some of my best advice.

"Thanks, man.", the brothers replied in unison.

"You know, we really don't know what our next stop will be," Abby admitted. "Any advice for us in return?"

"But the next place has to have surf," Gabe interjected.

"Funny you should mention that," Sam said. "Right before we came here, we spent a couple of weeks on Galveston Island. We'd been checking out Houston and thought we could head over there for some beach action. Anyway, they have a real surf cult there."

"Um… cult?" I asked, not quite understanding the reference.

"Sorry. I really should have said culture," Sam corrected. "Lots of the kids hang out with the surf crowd down there. They're pretty much the cool guys I guess. They party on the beach and listen to music. That sort of thing. But there are serious surfers there and we met some. You might want to head on down there for a bit."

Gabe's eyes lit up.

"What's on your mind, Gabe?", Sam queried.

"I once heard a guy say if you can surf Galveston you can surf anywhere. Might be worth a try.", Gabe responded sounding rather enthusiastic.

"Sold!" I exclaimed. "Maybe we can start planning tomorrow early."

"Well, plan on it taking a while," Jimmy offered. "It's over fifteen hundred miles from here. Took us like four days to get here."

"We take turns driving and maybe we can stop for a day in New Mexico or somewhere." Gabe suggested.

Sam turned his attention to Abby and asked, "Well cousin, what have you been up to?"

"I've been waiting tables mostly but someday I hope to end up being a writer," she replied.

"Cool! You mean like writing books?" he continued.

"No, more like newspaper reporting or maybe writing for a magazine."

"Wow. How do build the chops to do that?" Jimmy asked leaning forward, clearly impressed.

"Well for instance, I've been keeping a journal for a while. In fact, that's one reason I agreed to go on this little adventure. I think there are some neat things to write about out there.", Abby smiled at Jimmy's interest in her plans.

"You mean you're writing down what happens every day?" Gabe asked.

"No, not everything. Just the interesting stuff. I might even write it from a dog's perspective." She laughed again.

"Maybe you could call it *Skipper's Trip*," Gabe suggested.

"I'll think about it," she replied.

The next morning, we got up and decided to take Skipper for a long walk and look for breakfast.

Fortunately, we found a little place with an outdoor patio that would allow dogs, assuming they were well behaved. We assured the waitress our boy was, but none of us had any confidence in that promise.

After ordering our breakfasts, we began talking about the potential trip down to the Texas coast.

"It'll be a long haul," I said, "but there isn't much water between here and there unless we head down to Mexico."

"Man, I'd rather see the states before doing another country," Gabe said. "After all, I haven't been on the mainland that long."

We quickly agreed and vowed to find somewhere we could buy a map, so we could plan an interesting route.

That day we all went our separate ways and did a little sightseeing. Abby took responsibility for Skipper, so Gabe and I were free to roam around. When we got back to the motel that evening Gabe produced a map. Turns out he'd asked the desk clerk where to find one and the guy said he would loan us one if we promised to give it back.

Gabe had poured over the map and plotted out a potential route for us. He convinced us that if we didn't worry about how long it took we could stop by Phoenix and El Paso on the way. We decided to follow his advice, plan some side trips and noodle our way over to Galveston in our own time.

Luckily, Gabe's instincts proved correct and we really enjoyed the stopovers. We even ended up going up to the mountains above Phoenix to a magical place called Sedona. The red rock formations and big expansive sky above them really left an impression on me. Skipper loved the wide-open spaces and Abby let him run free every chance she got. I'm not really a spiritual person but I felt something in that little mountain top town and vowed to return. I'm sure Abby got a bunch of material for her journal there.

El Paso turned out to be a nice place to visit and we ended up finding a couple of rooms at a motel there. I was impressed by the Mexican influence on the town and enjoyed the food. Even though I was from southern California, I didn't have much experience with traditional Mexican cooking. It was eye opening. At one restaurant, we had the opportunity to meet the cook. His name was Jesus. Obviously, he pronounced it differently, but we were surprised by the spelling. Nice guy. He explained the different spices and ways to cook Mexican food and we left feeling as though we'd made a new friend.

It took just over a week to get to Galveston and it was worth every minute of the trip. Abby ended up getting a cold, but she was a trouper and never really complained, unless you consider the frequent sneezing. But by the time we got to our island destination it was under control.

Jimmy and Sam were right about the surf culture in Galveston. It wasn't long before I asked enough questions to find the best spots to put in my board. I quickly learned there was quite a story to be told there. I have my version and I'm sure Abby has hers.

The adventure continued.

Chapter Four

THE TREASURE ISLAND SURF CLUB (WHO KNEW?)

I have to admit that the only thing I knew about Galveston before we arrived was they had a devastating hurricane in 1900. I'd seen pictures of the aftermath and hoped I would never encounter that sort of surf. Another one called Carla hit in 1961 but by then the town was somewhat more prepared. None-the-less, that one did a lot of damage as well.

We finally pulled into Galveston about five PM one evening and first set about the task of finding somewhere to stay, preferably near the ocean. Galveston Island wasn't the tourist magnet that Las Vegas was, but there were still a number of motels available to accommodate the visitors that did come to enjoy the Gulf of Mexico, mostly people from Houston. We found a place across from the ocean called Gulf Shores Motel on 33rd Street at the seawall and ponied up for a couple of rooms. The motel had a multi-day discount, so we committed to a five day stay. Skipper was no problem since the motel advertised as dog friendly.

Gabe wanted to explore right away so the three of us… oops, the four of us, sorry Skipper…headed out for a walking tour of the beach front. We couldn't have found a better spot to survey the break since the most famous surfing spot on the water there in Galveston was at 37th Street. In fact, as we approached that area we noticed a dozen or so surfers enjoying the late day waves. Unfortunately, my board was back at the motel and after driving most of the day I wasn't in the mood to retrieve it. My first try at surfing in Texas would have to come tomorrow.

As we walked along the water's edge, I noticed several boards with the name 'Fry' written on them. Later in our stay, I'd have the good fortune of meeting a really interesting guy named Henry Fry, who at that time had virtually cornered the market on building ridable boards.

I have to say that we tried our best to meet some surfers that first evening, but most of our attempts were met with distrust. One exception was a longhaired kid named Joey. He was only fifteen or sixteen, but more than willing to tell us about the surfing crowd in that part of Texas. The kid was a dead ringer for David Marks of the Beachboys, or so I thought at the time. Cool hair and a bit of swagger, to the extent a teenager could have swagger.

"Don't be bummed by the other kids," Joey said when we asked about the chilly reception. "They're used to dealing with local rednecks who would rather kick your ass than shake your hand," he went on.

Turns out there was a healthy distrust between the surfers and their cowboy hat-wearing neighbors. Might have been because the surfers seemed to impress the girls, some of them the girlfriends of the 'townies', who idolized rodeo stars, football heroes and stock car racers.

"So how do the surfers feel about guys from California?" I asked.

"Some guys aren't too cool with it, but mostly because we're kind of in awe of you guys since your surf is huge compared to ours.", Joey replied, perfectly executing the hair flip so many guys did then.

Somehow, I didn't think the other guys in the surf crowd would agree with that explanation, but I really appreciated Joey's honesty.

"Can you introduce us around?" I asked Joey.

"Sure, although I'm kind of the little brother around here".

Joey zeroed in on some of the better-known guys, the ones he had the courage to approach or big-brothered him. One guy we really enjoyed meeting was Jimmy Rawlinson. Even though he'd grown up in Lubbock, he cut his surfing teeth in Hawaii while stationed there in the Air Force. In fact, while living there he was taught by his roommate Butch Van Artsdalen, a truly legendary big wave surfer.

Gabe and I were in awe of guys like Jimmy, but quite frankly Abby couldn't have cared less, even when we tried to explain the significance of their achievements. Skipper just yawned of course.

We also met a kid named Skip Walsh. He told the funniest story about his first experience surfing. Seems like he and a buddy started off two to a board. Now there's a trick. We almost busted a gut laughing but Skip (the boy not the dog) swore they never knew any better, particularly since his first boards were huge.

Most of the other people we met that first day or so were just wannabes from Houston, but I have to say that we actually felt welcomed by most of the crew on the beach.

Early the next day, I decided enough dry land was enough and had to find some surf or go crazy. Abby decided to hang back in her room and write, but Gabe and I headed to the beach around 37th to see how ridable the waves were that day.

When we got there Gabe said, "I don't know, Corky, these waves look pretty small, do you think you can even catch a ride?"

"Gabe, my boy, a real surfer can find a wave anywhere there's salt water," I replied, doubting my own words.

As luck would have it, after paddling out a good way, I ended up sitting on my board for a while before a wave came along worth riding. But I made the most of it and cruised on back to the beach having had a reasonably long ride. At least I got wet again and I felt pretty lucky to be back in a beachfront community.

Joey found us after a while and we asked him if the surf ever improved. He said, "You know this is no North Shore and I hope you didn't expect it to be, but it picks up on and off. Just a matter of being here when it does, man."

At that point I had nothing but patience. Over the next few days things did improve, and I had some really decent rides. I'd grown to like Galveston a lot and learned about a group of surfers called Treasure Island Surf Club. I think it was formed almost as a way to face the opposition – the older folks, football players and so forth who thought surfers were just, like I said earlier, beach bums. It gave a little structure to the culture but also provided a great excuse to party with friends.

We were never actually accepted into that group, but once they knew I was a legitimate surfer, we did have the chance to join in on some of the partying.

It was now July of 1966 and there was quite a buzz about a movie playing in Houston called *Endless Summer*. Up to that point, any movie featuring surfing was a goofy beach party movie. According to most people, this one gave a true accounting of the real art behind my sport. Naturally we had to see it.

So, one Saturday afternoon Gabe, Joey and I piled into the Buggy and headed up to Houston and the theater where the promising movie was playing. Again, Abby decided against joining us. You have to remember that the surfing culture wasn't one she had much interest in. Don't get me wrong, she understood the draw for me but had other priorities. I was a bit concerned that she either missed Half Moon Bay or Bennie's or just wanted to keep moving. I vowed to talk with her about it soon.

When we got to the theater expecting to get into a matinee, we were shocked. The place was jammed, and people were milling around outside. Everyone there looked like they just came from the beach. Long haired guys mixed with long haired girls. Everyone had a tan. Guess we should have figured.

"Jeez, Corky, what do we do now?" Gabe asked.

"I don't think we have much of a choice. Let's catch a burger and head back to the beach."

Joey chuckled and said, "That's a good idea. Based on this turnout, the beach won't be crowded."

As luck would have it, Joey was right. The beach was not nearly as crowded as normal and the surf was conveniently very ridable. Joey and I were able to catch quite a few good waves that day while Gabe appeared to snooze on the beach. Oh well, everyone has their priorities.

After Joey and I had surfed for a couple of hours, we pulled our boards out of the water and sat down to rest and enjoy the view.

"Joey, I've been meaning to ask you. You're pretty young to be hanging around down here, aren't you? What do your parents say?"

Joey seemed reluctant to talk about his situation but finally blurted out, "My folks live in Dallas. I don't think they know where I am actually."

"Dude, they must be worried to death!", I said, I'm sure looking surprised.

"I don't know. I don't think so. I call them every once in a while and let'em know I'm okay."

"Aren't they looking for you?"

"No probably not, dunno."

"Wow, Joey, what does your dad do anyway?".

"He, uh...smokes.", Joey said casting a glance toward the water. I think I saw a couple of tears at that point.

I knew immediately what he meant and didn't pursue it any further for that moment.

"So, I see you on the beach every day but where do you live?"

"Mainly on the beach. Sometimes I crash with one of the other surfers."

"Where did you get money for a board anyway?" I asked, assuming correctly that he had no money or job.

"A guy named Lee had one that was used and just gave it to me, at least to use."

Turns out Lee was another well-known surfer from the area and a good guy.

"Well that's super. You deserve it, man. But hey…it's late. Let's go get something to eat.", I said, stomach grumbling.

Gabe was awake now and we all headed back to the motel to find Abby and head out for some food. Abby was waiting for us and ravenous. Skipper was fed and walked and we all headed out to look for something interesting. We found a little Italian place that Abby noticed offered a veggie plate along with all the meaty spaghetti, lasagna sort of things.

We bought Joey a nice dinner and all enjoyed the really spicy tomato sauce. Abby rated the vegetable plate as only okay, but at least she found something she could eat. As we left the restaurant, Joey said goodnight and headed off, turning down our offer to let him crash in Gabe and my room. I felt guilty but wasn't really qualified to 'parent' Joey.

Next morning, I got out of bed early to catch some quick waves before breakfast and an agreed upon powwow to talk about next steps. I'd heard about a competition coming up the following weekend that actually had some prize money. Based on what I'd seen on Galveston island, I thought I had a fair chance of doing well. I asked Gabe and Abby to bear with me and agree to stay until after that event. Both agreed, with Abby doing so less enthusiastically.

As the week went on, I looked for Joey but sort of lost track of him. I was worried I have to admit but believed that Joey was one smart little dude who could probably take care of himself. On the Friday before the competition, I ran into the guy Lee who had fronted Joey a board. After talking for a while, he told me that Joey had left town and he thought headed to Dallas. I really hoped that was the case. Good kid. Maybe his goodness would rub off on his parents.

On the morning of the competition, I arrived about forty-five minutes before registration, did some stretching and finally approached the registration table to get my number. Looking around, I found myself being really grateful not to see Nat or David or Corky Carroll standing there. Maybe I had a chance.

Unfortunately, they couldn't have picked a worse day for this event. It was hard to catch a ride and when you did, the wave sort of fizzled. All of that actually worked to my advantage, though, and I won my first minor competition and a little money…although not much.

Gabe and Abby and even Skipper had been on the beach rooting me on. At least I thought I saw Skipper rooting me on. Ya never know.

I came back to where they were and apologized for the lousy surf, like I had any influence.

"You know, maybe it was for the best," Abby offered, "One of my problems with surfing is seeing really bad wipeouts. I stopped watching surfers because I was always afraid one of them would get hurt."

"I think the only way you could get hurt today is for someone to throw a rock at you from the beach." I chuckled.

"Or stub a toe on a pilon." Gabe added.

"Anyway, congratulations King Corky!" Abby said, giving me a hug.

Soon, a few other surfers had come by to slap my hand and tell me they looked forward to beating my butt the next time. I didn't tell them there might not be a next time there in Galveston. I had a feeling I might return, but out of respect I knew I had to get ready to move on with my traveling companions.

I don't think I ever encountered a more committed surfing community outside of the obvious big wave places. These guys and girls were totally into promoting the surfing lifestyle in this little island town and had begun to win converts, even among the cowboys.

We were packing up the following Monday when we were surprised to see Joey walking up the street towards us.

"Wow, Joey, we thought you were gone forever," I said.

"No, man, I can't stay away from this place."

"Where have you been for the past week?", I asked, not trying to hide my concern.

"Well, I decided to head to Dallas to see my folks."

"So how did that go?" Gabe asked.

"Better than I thought. I told them I loved my life here but would check back in once in a while. I'm not going back to school in the fall. Maybe I'll get a certificate later, but not right now."

"How did they take it?" I asked, waiting for what I thought would be an explosive response.

"All my dad sad was 'far out'."

Such was life in the 60s.

Chapter Five

THE BIG UNEASY

We left Galveston with the general thought of heading for another gulf surfing spot. One of the Treasure Island guys had told us there was some good surf near Gulf Shores, Alabama, so we headed east with the hope of finding some bigger waves and maybe another competition or two where my experience would pay off.

Once we were under way, Abby and Skipper snoozed in the back seat of the Buggy while Gabe perused the road map he never got around to returning. As he mapped out our route, I started thinking about Joey.

"You know Gabe, that Joey is a smart kid and will probably be fine, but I felt funny just leaving him behind."

"You know we couldn't bring him with us, Corky. There are laws," Gabe replied, as if he had direct knowledge.

"That's not what I was thinking, but at least we could have left him some cash or something."

"I told you that you should let me sit at the tables in Vegas a bit longer. Right now, we need all the bread we have.

In fact, pretty soon we'll have to find a way to win or work for some more," Gabe said, wincing when he said, 'work for'.

"I slipped him a fifty." We heard Abby say.

"I didn't know you were awake," I said.

"Gee, Abby, I wish you'd have asked us before you did that," Gabe whined.

"No, Gabe, it's okay. I think Abby did the right thing and it makes me feel better actually."

"Whatever you say, but we're getting a little low."

"You're a regular den mother, Abby," I kidded.

"Well I kind of know what he's going through I guess.", Abby said under her breath.

That didn't seem like an odd comment at the time but later I wondered what she meant.

Gabe had done his homework and convinced us to follow Route 82, so we could stay near the gulf. We figured we could then spend some time in New Orleans just for the experience. So, we'd worked our way over to Port Arthur to pick up that route. We were told it could be a pretty desolate stretch of highway, but that the scenery was good, and we would encounter some beachfront along the way. We topped off the gas and kept moving.

We finally crossed into Louisiana and were making good time on our nine or ten hour trip when I noticed a car coming up quickly behind us. It caught my eye partly because it was a Plymouth almost the same year as the Buggy.

As I'm sure you guessed, soon a red light started flashing. I looked at Gabe and saw that he was growing nervous, so I tried to stay cool.

"No problem, my man. We're clean," I said. "No cause for concern."

I carefully pulled the Buggy over and fished my drivers' license out of my pocket, anticipating the policeman's request.

As the officer approached the car, I noticed that he was a heavy-set man, probably in his fifties whose belly hung low over his belt, even though there was clearly a gun hanging there too. He wore a sort of cowboy hat and sunglasses, making him look even more ominous.

"Afternoon, folks, how ya'll today?" he asked.

"Doing well officer," I said in my best middle America accent.

The policeman peered into the car, tipping his sunglasses forward.

"You folks some sort of hippie band?"

Obviously, we did look a bit odd at this point. One white guy with shaggy hair (see like I told Abby, we're getting there), a Hawaiian who sometimes looked as wide as he did tall and a red headed cheerleader in the back seat with a scruffy little dog. I almost chuckled under my breath but decided it best to stifle it.

"No sir, not a rock band."

"Um, hmm... I see ya'll have California plates. Long way from home, ain't ya?"

"Yes sir, just traveling around the country looking for places to put the board in."

"Come again?", the officer said, clearly confused.

"Oh sorry, officer, I mean places to surf."

"Try me again."

"That board on the top is a surf board. You take it into the ocean, stand on it and ride the waves back to the beach."

"You don't say?" said the officer, giving the board a good look. "Why in God's name would you want to do that?"

"It gives you one heck of a rush. Uh…I mean…makes you feel really good, makes you appreciate nature I guess," I said quickly, modifying my lingo.

"Um, hmm… Well, can I see your license and registration please.", the cop said returning to the business at hand.

"Yes, sir, but if I can ask, why did you pull us over?"

"You can ask."

That was that for the moment. The officer looked over my documentation and passed it back to me.

"Well, son, my name is Sheriff Rupert Girth. I'm the law around these parts."

Gabe tried hard to hold back a laugh but had some difficulty.

"Something funny, boy?" Sheriff Girth asked

"He's been coughing all day," Abby rushed to the rescue.

"Um, hm."

I was getting a little uncomfortable now, but things quickly took a turn for the better.

"Ya'll staying around here?", the sheriff changed the subject.

"It's beautiful country but we're on our way to Gulf Shores, Alabama."

"You don't say. I've been there. Beautiful part of the country but not as beautiful as Louisiana."

After another look around, Sheriff Girth continued, "I pulled you over just to be certain you kids weren't up to no good, but ya'll seem like good'uns to me."

"Thank you, officer," I said, very relieved.

"That's sheriff, son. Say, have you kids eaten today?"

"Just a quick breakfast when we left Galveston."

"Well I'll be, I've been there too. Anyway, my sister has a little place about a mile further on. Best fried catfish sandwiches around, if you want to have some lunch before you leave."

"Well that sounds really good to me," I said, looking at the others, who now seemed relieved as well.

"Tell you what, follow me and I'll show you right where it is.", Sheriff Girth suggested.

"Well that's the best way to drum up business I've ever seen," Abby said as the sheriff walked back to his car.

"Hell yes. Create a captive audience," Gabe said, still visibly shaking from the experience.

Soon, we pulled into the parking lot of a small roadside combination restaurant and gas station. We'd seen this sort of business along the way, but it never occurred to us to eat at a gas station. On the other hand, the smells coming out of the place were pretty inviting. I couldn't tell if it was barbeque or roast chicken or what, but it made my mouth water.

We all piled out of the car, leaving Skipper behind to continue his nap. He didn't protest even with the smells filling the car. Abby made sure to leave her windows down some to be certain Skip didn't get too warm. Sheriff Girth was parked beside us and got out of his cruiser, working hard to hoist up his pants as he did.

"Come on in and I'll introduce you to my sister."

The sign painted on the front window said *Annalee's Good Food*. I was hoping we could trust that claim. We all entered the small dining room. There were four small wooden tables in front of the windows facing the road and a row of seven or eight stools at the counter that had clearly seen better days. The red vinyl on the seats was cracked from years of use. This place was certainly nothing special, but it was clean, and the smells were making me again realize how hungry I was.

"Annalee, these kids are on a road trip and looking for... What was that again?"

"Places to surf," I said explaining to the sheriff's sister in much the same way I did with the sheriff.

"Folks, this is my sister, Annalee Robinson, best cook in the parish.", Sheriff Girth said with a great deal of pride.

Annalee was a pretty woman about thirty-five or forty with long brown hair pulled back into a pony tail. She seemed downright thin to me given that she owned a restaurant. But I've heard people say that if you own a bar you're better off being a teetotaler, if you catch my drift.

"Hi ya'll. Welcome to Annalee's," the sister said in a very heavy southern accent touched with what we came to find out was creole.

We all said our hellos and "pleased to meet yous" and decided to sit at the counter for lunch. We were a little surprised when the sheriff sat down beside us. Annalee brought us menus and I was impressed by how many selections she offered. That said, I thought it might be a good idea to order the catfish sandwich the sheriff recommended, even though I'd never tasted catfish and didn't eat much fried food anyway.

"Ma'am, the sheriff was bragging on your catfish sandwich, so I think I'll have one of those," I said.

Gabe and Abby looked me as if I was from Mars, but quickly picked up on the wisdom.

"I'll have the same, ma'am. Love catfish," Gabe said, knowing there was no truth to it.

Annalee was beaming that her signature creation was getting its due.

"How 'bout you, young lady…you want the same?", she said, anticipating another positive response.

Abby looked at me sheepishly but decided to hold her own.

"No, ma'am, I'm a vegetarian," she said, looking carefully at the menu for ideas.

"Well, I'll be," Annalee said "I don't think I ever met a vegetarian, how 'bout you, Rupert?"

"Can't say that I have, sister."

"Well no matter, I can fix up a vegetable plate if you like.", Annalee said, readily accepting the challenge.

Abby looked sincerely relieved. Annalee headed over to the grill to start lunch and Sheriff Girth stood up as if to leave.

"Well, ya'll enjoy your lunch. Hope you find somewhere to … How did you say that? Put in your board."

"Thanks so much, sheriff," I replied. "And thanks for the tip on where to have lunch," I said.

The sheriff shuffled out, again hiking up his trousers, and I felt certain he would head back to the same spot where we had encountered him so that he could charm travelers to his sister's restaurant. At that point, we didn't mind the delay at all. Having lunch at this little dive sure seemed better than dealing with a big traffic ticket or worse.

Soon, Annalee dished up our catfish sandwiches and to my surprise, mine was really tasty. It came with crispy French fries and a Coke. The drink was super cold, and I guzzled about half of it before I even took a bite of my lunch.

I looked at Gabe and saw that he was inhaling the sandwich, so I guessed he agreed that it was darned good. We were really surprised to find that Annalee had carefully prepared Abby a plate of steamed vegetables. She may never have met a vegetarian, but she clearly knew how to feed one. Abby was delighted.

"So, where are you kids headed from here?" Annalee asked.

"Well, like we told your brother, we're headed for the beach in Alabama but may stop for a bit in New Orleans," I replied.

"You know I always wanted to go to New Orleans but, even though I've lived in Louisiana all my life, I never had the chance."

"I guess it's never too late," I said as encouragingly as I could.

"I expect," she replied, looking down.

"I notice your name is Robinson," Abby ventured, "Does your husband work here with you?"

"No, hon, Mr. Robinson ran off a couple of years ago."

We let that drop in a flash. About that time, a young family came into the dining room followed closely by Sheriff Girth. The sheriff introduced everyone as best he could and headed back out. I guess our theory was correct. We finished our lunches and thanked Annalee sincerely, surprised at how much we had enjoyed the food and even her enthusiasm for serving us.

"If you ever come back this way," Annalee shouted out to us as we headed back to the car, "please come on back and see us."

We assured her we would, even though we knew the chances were pretty remote.

"Boy, that whole thing wasn't what I expected," Gabe said as we pulled out of the parking lot.

"I agree. There for a minute I thought we had driven into a bad situation. I wonder if everyone in the south is that friendly?" I asked. Turns out they weren't, but that's another story for another day.

I was itching to do some surfing again, but I soon realized both Gabe and Abby really wanted to experience New Orleans.

"Do you think we can agree to staying no longer than two days?" I ventured.

Both of my companions agreed, and we headed on to The Big Easy.

When we got to New Orleans, it was nearly eight o'clock in the evening and we were bushed. It turned out to be harder to find somewhere to stay than we anticipated. After trying a few motels on the outskirts of town and against our better judgement, we pulled over in a little park and tried to catch some sleep. I woke up the next morning and noticed Abby and Skipper weren't in the back seat, but that Gabe was still sleeping soundly. Of course, he could sleep through a hurricane, so that wasn't too comforting.

Concerned, I got out of the car and called out for Abby. I heard her voice in the distance and finally she and our pooch emerged from the woods near where we parked.

"Good morning!" she said in a more cheerful voice than she'd used in two or three days.

"Where have you guys been?" I asked.

"Just doing our business," she said, giggling.

"Oh..."

"What are we going to do about breakfast?" I asked.

"I know exactly," Abby replied. "We're going to find some beignets and coffee."

"What's a beignet?" I asked, feeling undereducated.

"It's a sort of doughnut that's famous here. You'll love 'em."

So, we woke Gabe and told him about our quest. He readily agreed, particularly with the prospect of finding hot coffee. We decided to head down towards the Mississippi River and look for breakfast. New Orleans is an old town. You could tell by the low-slung buildings and ancient churches. The entire town smelled like a combination of deep south cooking and beer. Not at all unpleasant.

We were impressed to see several bakeries and restaurants that advertised the doughy treat. Finally, we settled on Café du Monde. Someone later told us it had been there since the mid-1860s and had become the most famous beignet and coffee house in the city. Conveniently they had an outdoor deck and we sat down to enjoy another new food group.

Once the beignets and coffee were in front of us, we dug in and there were oohs and aahs from each of us. The coffee was strong and hot, and the beignets were lightly dusted and just the right temperature.

"Sorry guys, but I think I'm going to settle down here," Gabe said after his third roll.

Knowing he was kidding, I suggested we decide how we would spend our time in New Orleans so that we could get on with our journey. I needed to find water soon. Just couldn't imagine surfing on the Mississippi. I found out later there are actually spots to surf around that part of Louisiana and that some people even surfed on Lake Pontchartrain. But I was looking for some larger waves.

We all agreed that the big draw in New Orleans was Bourbon Street. Later that morning, we managed to find a little motel near where we'd slept the night before and checked in for one night. The little lady behind the counter in the office even volunteered to babysit Skipper. She was clearly a dog person, as we noticed what appeared to be a little Scottie sleeping on the floor. We gratefully accepted and headed for Bourbon Street.

We got there about dark after a light dinner at a burger shop. I don't think we were prepared for what we saw. The crowds were thick, and people were walking around with drinks in hand right there in the middle of the street. Music blared from every bar and club we encountered as we walked along. The road was cobblestone and we noticed people that had clearly been drinking a while stumbling while trying to navigate the uneven pavement.

A little black boy approached us and spoke directly to Gabe. "Hey man, I betcha a dolla I'kin tell you where you gots those shoes.", he said with confidence.

"No chance", Gabe said with equal bravado.

"Den is it a bet?", the little boy said smiling and sticking out his hand to shake Gabe's.

"You bet", Gabe said appropriately.

"You gots dem shoes on yo feet", the young con artist said.

Gabe rolled his eyes in disbelief and mumbled under his breath but quickly produced a "dolla". He'd been had and he knew it. Abby and I could hardly stop laughing.

"Guys, let's just pick one of these places and have a drink," I suggested.

So, we randomly picked out a bar that was open to the street. On stage was band playing music like I'd never heard before. One guy played a harmonica, another had what looked like a washboard on his chest. The singer had a bluesy voice, but the music was anything but down and out blues. It was something completely different. *How bizarre,* I thought. I saw a sign that identified the band and the Zydeco Kings. I had no idea what Zydeco was but decided to research it later.

We sat there for an hour or so and sipped our drinks. No one had asked us for identification and we didn't offer any. *Must be pretty lax about drinking age*, I thought to myself.

Finally, Abby tugged on my sleeve and managed to shout over the music. "We should get back."

Clearly this scene wasn't for her. I think Gabe was enjoying himself, but I favored her point of view.

We headed back to the motel and ended up getting a really good night's sleep. The next morning, we decided to have one more breakfast of beignets and coffee. The lady behind the motel counter suggested a place two doors down that we hadn't noticed before. We sat at a picnic table, wolfed down our breakfast and bought an extra bag of the magical pastries and stopped back by the motel.

"Ma'am we thank you such much for looking after our little friend," Abby said to the lady behind the desk, genuinely appreciating the gesture. "Don't know if you've had breakfast but we brought you some beignets. The man said eat 'em while their hot."

"Oh, I know, honey", the desk clerk said opening the bag and inhaling the sweet smell. "Thank ya'all so much!".

We all agreed we were glad to have experienced New Orleans but that our goal was to see the country while finding surfing spots. So, off we went looking for white sand and big waves. Our next stop was to provide both.

Laissez le bon temp rouler.

Let the good times roll!

Chapter Six

SURF, SAND AND MISSING ALMA

As we headed back out onto the highway, we discussed how amazed we were at the different cultures we'd encountered so far. From the renegade surf community in Galveston to the free-wheeling party crowd on Bourbon Street. From Joey, the young runaway from Dallas, to the salesman/sheriff in a little town in Louisiana, to his talented entrepreneur and short order cook sister, to the sweet little lady who proved to be a great dog sitter. And we all agreed that experiencing southern cooking was pretty eye opening. I think I knew I'd become a catfish convert and I know Gabe was already craving his next beignet. But it was time to find a break, not to mention some way to make some money.

It took us a few more hours to work our way around to the Gulf Shores area in Alabama. A local pointed us to Orange Beach. He wasn't able to tell us whether there was decent surf there but did tell us most folks interested in the Gulf ended up in that area. Seemed a logical place to start.

Orange Beach did turn out to be a great stretch of white sand. It looked to us as though there was a pretty healthy tourist trade. Similar to Galveston, which drew its tourists from nearby Houston, Orange Beach was a getaway for folks from Birmingham. There were some traditional oceanfront motels and attractions, but you could tell the area was transitioning from a little town on the ocean to a place to go for sun and sand.

From a surfing standpoint being in a tourist destination could be a good thing or a bad thing. Sometimes in peak season the beaches got so crowded that surfing was pretty dangerous for both the surfers and the sun worshipers. But the tourists also spent money and that meant there were shops that catered to surfers and tourists alike. Surveying the beach to assess the break, we quickly saw that the water was pretty glassy. So, we continued to drive around until we found an outdoor burger and dog joint where we noticed a couple of dogs. Canine dogs not hot dogs. So, we knew Skipper would be cool.

Being super hungry, we piled out of the Buggy and found a table with a pretty nice water view. Abby seemed a bit more mellow than she had in the past few days, a development that I found encouraging. Ever since we left Half Moon Bay, I'd seemed to detect some sadness or maybe depression, but I couldn't for the life of me figure out what might have been the cause, unless she did miss her life back there.

A young, long-haired waiter approached us and welcomed us to *The Beach Hut*. He looked to be about our age, so I thought he might clue us in on the surfing scene in the area.

"Hey guys, what's up?" he asked. "My name's Jamie and I'll take care of you today. Wanna beer or something stronger?"

Abby ordered a soda (hey that's what they called them in the south) and Gabe and I ordered Budweiser's. Once again, there was no attempt to card us, but this time I suspected it was because Jamie was one of us. No matter, a cold one was going to taste really good after our drive.

After delivering our drinks and us having reviewed the limited menu, Jamie asked if we wanted some lunch.

"Ladies first," I said, knowing Abby was struggling with finding something she could eat.

"Gee thanks, Corky!" she came back. "Well, I'm a vegetarian, Jamie, what would you suggest?"

"Far out. Me too!" Jamie seemed pleased. "It's not on the menu but the cook knows how to make something he calls a vegaburger."

"Never heard of it," Abby said. "But looks like I'm going to try one. Some slaw too."

"Uh, Jamie, what in the world is in a vegaburger?" I ventured.

"Beats the hell out of me but I eat 'em and I'm still here," he replied with a toothy grin.

Now there's a solid recommendation, I thought to myself. *I eat our cook's food and I'm still alive.* Jeez.

Gabe and I ordered a chili dog and fries and Abby immediately sniffed in disapproval.

"Well, Abby, I've been eating hot dogs most of my life and I'm still alive," I chuckled, paraphrasing Jamie. He just stood there looking, well, clueless.

Soon, we were served our lunches and Abby reported that the vegetarian burger wasn't half bad. I suppose that meant it wasn't half good either but kept it to myself.

When Jamie came back to check on us, I asked if he knew where you went for surfing in the area. For some reason, the way he looked seemed to shout 'surfer', but that wasn't the case. He did say he knew some guys that might be able to help us find a place. Two brothers named Al and Arnie 'something or other' (his words) ran a water sports rental place a little further down the beach.

After we paid our tab, we headed off to find the 'something or other brothers. It wasn't difficult to locate the rental hut. There was loud music playing and big sign saying, *Beach Fun Starts Here.*

As we approached, we heard a guy behind the counter haggling with what looked to be a dad trying to rent a float for his kid. I quickly gathered that the dad made the case it was late in the day and most places discounted for a shorter period of rental.

"But not us", the young man replied with what seemed to be a strong Northeast accent. Maybe New York or Philly. I only knew that accent from growing up watching way too much tv. Finally, the dad relented so as not to disappoint his son and the guy behind the counter smiled as they walked away as if he'd won a significant battle.

We approached the dude and told him Jamie at The Beach Hut said he might help us with our quest. The guy was late teens, early twenties, with a dark complexion and wavy brown hair.

"He's a dork," the guy responded. "Anyway, my name is Al and that guy schlepping the rafts over there is my brother

Arnie," he said. "What can I tell ya or sell ya?" There was that accent again.

"Actually, we're looking for somewhere with decent surf," I explained, even as Al's eyes were scoping Abby fairly obviously. Abby looked at him as if he was a bug.

"Man, are you in the wrong place," Al said, softening his approach and accent. "I don't know what you've heard or why you came here but the surf here can be a tragedy. My brother and I gave up a long time ago."

"Oh, so you guys surf?" I asked.

"Hell yes, man, what else is there?"

"So, where do you go?"

At which time Arnie walked up, heard our discussion and piped up. "We head over to Florida when we are seriously looking for a ride." Arnie was obviously Al's twin. I couldn't imagine how anyone other than family could tell them apart.

"The guys over there are the real deal. Couple of guys have national reps. Guys like Yancey Spencer.", Arnie continued.

That was a name I hadn't heard before, but I made a mental note to look him up if we decided to head to Florida.

"So, you can't catch a ride at all here?" I asked. I was starting to think we had gotten some bad advice.

"Well, sometimes on Dauphin Island but you may be sitting on your board a while before a decent one comes along."

Because there were tourists coming up to rent floats and tubes, we were able to learn a bit more about the brothers. Originally, they were from Philadelphia but had come down to Gulf Shores a few times with their folks and fell in love with the beach. They had learned to surf on Long Island of all places and naturally assumed they would find a break here. As disappointed as that reality was, they decided to stay and try to make a living working the tourist trade.

After talking a bit more, we found out their last name wasn't 'something or other' at all but Ignazio. Their family was pretty well to do and didn't approve of the beach life. But the brothers had assured them they would settle down and maybe head to college after a break (no pun intended). That was three years ago.

"So, what's the name of your hut?" I asked.

"It's right there, dude. *Beach Fun Starts Here,*" Al said proudly. I was thinking it was no General Motors, but I guess it described the business pretty well.

The brothers managed to give us as much time and advice as they could but finally had to wrap up for the day. We offered to buy them a beer, but they had other plans and begged off. We thanked them, shook hands (Al lingering a bit with Abby) and headed on down the beach to talk about what we'd learned.

"Damn, I think we may have a bit of a dilemma," I worried out loud. "Should we try Dauphin Island or head on over to Florida?" Al and Arnie had given us pretty good directions to the Pensacola area and a couple of names of guys to look up.

"So Corky, I think we just keep moving," Gabe said, "You need to find the right surf break, or you'll likely melt like the wicked witch."

"I agree," Abby said. "Anyway, I've always wanted to visit Florida, so let's head on."

That night we didn't bother finding a room. There was a parking lot adjacent to the beach that seemed a little quiet. There were even public restrooms where we could freshen up and change clothes, so we just hunkered down for a few winks before heading out the next morning.

Turned out that the drive from Orange Beach to Pensacola only took an hour, and the directions the brothers had given us were right on.

About ten minutes before we anticipated crossing the state line, Gabe looked at me and said, "What if you needed a little thing to get into Florida and we didn't have it?" He actually seemed serious.

"You really haven't traveled much have you, Gabe? Jeez."

"Just wondered," he said, sheepishly. Guess Gabe and I would need to have a chat.

We got to our destination mid-morning and right away headed to the beach to find the surf, or at least someone to tell us where to look. While there were some surfers sitting on their boards when we got to the water, ridable waves were few and far between. One guy apparently gave up and headed back to the beach.

I walked up to him and asked if he could point us to a decent break. Looking at me warily, he told me he was new to the area but that our best bet was to head over the Hutson's Hardware and Surf Shop. He had recently been stationed in Pensacola with the military and himself had been looking for a place to routinely enjoy a decent ride. He told me he had heard other surfers mention the place as a sort of focal point of Florida Gulf surf culture. I thanked him, and we set out to find the only hardware and surf shop I'd ever heard of. Nuts, bolts and surfwax. Hmmm.

The shop turned out to be pretty far from the beach. We walked in to find a fair number of what appeared to be surfers milling around and talking the language. They were mixed in with some older locals, who were there to get materials for do it yourself projects. Odd mix but everyone seemed pretty mellow.

We began asking around about finding a break and finally found a guy named Kelly who seemed to know what he was talking about. Don't know if Kelly was his first name or last but he just introduced himself as 'Kelly'. Kelly told us the best break in the area was around the pier. We knew that was often the case, but some breaks are better than others.

"Is the surf fairly reliable?" I asked.

"Well yeah, but you may have to paddle out a number of times to catch a really good wave. Couple of weeks ago we caught some great rides. Hurricane Alma hit over by Apalachee Bay and kicked up some good breaks even over here."

I was now regretting spending so much time on dry land.

"Some of the guys headed over there to get near the landfall. Said it was awesome!", Kelly continued, clearly disappointed he hadn't made it there himself.

"Darn, sorry we missed it".

"It was only a minor storm by hurricane standards when it hit, but the waves ran ten or twelve feet over that way, maybe six and sometimes seven here."

We thanked Kelly for the heads up. He gave us some directions to get us on our way back to the right area of the beach near the pier. By this time, I was really feeling the need for salt water. It had been way too long.

As luck would have it, the surf was breaking nicely when we arrived, and I wasted no time heading out. As usual, Gabe set up camp on the beach to check out the local talent. Abby decided to walk Skipper along the water's edge to give me some time and space.

I was able to catch several really nice waves that I could ride all the way in. I was pretty amazed at how consistent they were, contrary to the warning Kelly gave us.

When I came out of the water later in the day I was exhausted. Bad sign. I knew I had to get in more surfing to make sure I wasn't losing my touch or my stamina.

Luckily, we found a motel to park for a day or two. I had decided to keep on surfing the pier for a couple of days anyway and meanwhile we could decide our next stop. A guy at a burger joint near our motel suggested Daytona Beach on the Atlantic side. He had surfed there and recommended a couple of spots.

After two days of catching as many waves as I could, we decided to set our sights on Daytona as our next stop.

Florida had been good to us so far and things would get even better.

Chapter Seven

ANOTHER DAY, ANOTHER PIER

It was four hundred fifty or so miles from where we were in Pensacola to Daytona and we figured it would take us most of a day to get there, but we were determined to make it before dark. We started our journey early on a Friday morning and weaved our way through the small towns and tourist traps for about five hours before stopping for a quick lunch.

Abby was in luck this time since we found a roadside vegetable market that also had a little lunch stand. In addition to sandwiches served with potato chips, they would fix you anything you wanted with the fresh vegetables. Abby ordered two ears of perfectly cooked corn and a salad. Gabe and I ended up with our usual questionable choices, but all of us left happy.

We arrived in Daytona around four o'clock that afternoon and were directed to the area around the pier to look for a surf spot. Kinda figured. By now I had determined that you always look for the pier first, at least everywhere outside of California.

The pier ran off of a boardwalk that had an amusement park area. It also had several shops and arcades to draw in the tourists. Abby said she thought it looked creepy since guys were stationed at the doors of the arcades to try to beckon you in. I guess I could see her point.

Gabe was determined to explore the attractions and headed off with a few dollars in his pocket to satisfy his curiosity. We had learned days ago to let Abby hold the money. Otherwise, Gabe would find a card game, slot machine, group of guys playing craps or some other means of depleting our funds. Or at least that was our theory. I went along with it because, well, Abby was right in suggesting it.

Of course, by this time money had become an issue. All three of us realized that we had to find some way of increasing our stash or our little adventure would grind to a halt. We decided to stay in Daytona for several days to try to find a way to make some cash.

Abby was determined to leverage her experience waiting tables and relatively quickly found a job in a little beachside bar that specialized in shrimp. While the hourly wage wasn't much, Abby had a way of impressing the customers enough to come home with a good day of tips. I'd learned that back in Half Moon Bay. I, on the other hand, had never made as much waiting tables at Bennies. I suspect it was because I didn't know how to 'chat up' the clientele as Abby called it. So, waiting tables didn't seem the best way for me to contribute.

My idea was to find the closest shop catering to surfers and surf wannabes and play up my "vast experience" surfing the west coast. At least I knew the lingo and could talk a good game. I found a little place right on the tourist strip called Jack's Surf and Sail and walked in determined to get a job.

"Is the manager around?" I asked to a guy maybe thirty years old. He had shoulder length hair and was wearing a muscle shirt with *Surf Naked* written on it. Now there's a sight.

"I'm the owner," he replied, sticking out this hand. I incorrectly expected a regular handshake but realized he intended the "brother shake". I corrected as quickly as I could, and we got caught sort of in between. But he just laughed.

"The name's Andy," he said with a slight accent of some sort.

"Uh, but the shop is named Jack's," I said, stating the obvious.

"Yep. You got me there. What can I do for you?"

I introduced myself and let him know I was looking for work and had a great deal of experience (not really telling him at what, of course). Instead I emphasized the fact that I was a surfer from California. I must admit I embellished the background story in that my wins in events on the West Coast were somewhat overstated. Okay, have it your way, *grossly* overstated. I was a little surprised that he didn't seem too impressed.

"Well, Corky. Is that your name? Surfing the East Coast is a different bear. Not sure how you can recommend a board or a break or anything, being from California and all."

"I'm a pretty quick study. Anyway, maybe a bit different perspective could be valuable. Did I tell you I surfed Hawaii?" I asked, padding my resume again.

"You willing to work on commission?"

"Sure. at least until I prove myself."

"Done deal," Andy said, reaching out his hand again. This time we successfully executed the brother shake. After discussing my commission percentage and my shift, Andy showed me around the shop and familiarized me with his merchandise. Nothing too exotic. He had a mix of things for surfers but also a decent array of t-shirts and so forth that would appeal to the tourist trade.

Over the next few days, I got to know the area and the local surf crowd fairly well. I also figured out a way to spin my stories of big waves, beach parties and surfer girls to the extent that I was selling a fair amount of surf gear and even an occasional board. But I really seemed to appeal to the tourists. It's as if they had never encountered anyone from California, much less Hawaii before. Even the moms and dads who brought in their teenagers seemed to be impressed with my little stories of fame and glory.

While I was reaching some manner of star status, I also realized I had sort have become a parody of myself, but then I was making very good money. That combined with Abby's wages and tips was beginning to mount up. Meanwhile, Gabe was having difficulty finding anything that suited him. Not that he didn't try. He just didn't seem to find his groove. So much for the gift of Gabe. Abby and I decided not to make too much of an issue of it. At least he wasn't spending his day sleeping on the beach.

I usually spent the morning surfing and went to work around one in the afternoon, working through early evening when the tourists were wandering up and down the strip after a day at the beach. I thought my surfing skills were improving. In that part of Florida, the waves broke to the right and I was getting used to reading the ocean and picking out just the right wave.

After being in Daytona for about ten days, Andy told me about a competition the following weekend down by the pier. His shop was one of the sponsors and he thought it would be good for business if I signed up to compete. I found out they called it the South Atlantic Surfing Championship. Of course, I'd never heard of it and suspected it was a grand name for a minor event but decided to compete and try to represent Jack's as well as I could. I convinced myself that my surfing skills were at least somewhat advanced compared to the locals and that I was helping both Jack's and me if I could pull off a win.

The other sponsors were mostly local hangouts and one radio station. I did notice that Hobie was represented on the banner they had staked out on the beach. I'd definitely heard that name before so I filed it away in my brain. I'd find out more about that sponsor later.

On the day of the event, I pulled the Buggy right down onto the beach. At Daytona you could drive up and down a long stretch of beach and even park your car there during daylight hours. As I was pulling my board down from the Buggy I noticed something interesting. I was a longboard rider. Looking around I noticed a fair number of much shorter boards. Even though I'd seen a few at the shop, I was still quite surprised to see so many in the competition.

Andy came walking down the beach and asked if I was ready to kick some butt. I mentioned to him my surprise at the number of shorter boards.

"They're starting to become more popular for sure, but this break favors the longboard most days," he said, surveying the other competitors. "Pretty soon I want to start designing and making some boards of my own, maybe with the Jack's logo. We'll see."

"You know, looking at the registrations I noticed a bunch of these guys aren't the usual local crowd", he continued, "Some are from other areas of the state. Even a couple from the Caribbean. Don't know what that means exactly but it's a little odd for this type of gig."

I wasn't sure what to make of that either.

Soon the horn sounded, and the competitors gathered near a lifeguard stand to hear the details of the competition. Andy had me wearing a Jack's Surf and Sail t-shirt with my competitor number on the back for the event. I wasn't used to wearing a shirt while surfing at all and it felt downright weird. My number was – eighteen. My age.

I had several really good rides early on, but the competition was a lot more seasoned than I imagined. My last wave of the day crested and curled perfectly, and I entered the tube for a good while before popping out to a bunch of cheers. I thought it was for some local hero, but it turned out to be for me and my ride. I rode the wave on into the beach and stepped off of my board. I was feeling pretty confident at that point.

Sure enough, I took first place, largely because of the reaction to the last ride I'm certain. I thought I was just lucky to catch that particular wave and hang on, but Andy and Gabe convinced me I looked like one of my West Coast idols coming out.

The purse was two hundred fifty dollars for the winner. That seemed like a fortune to me and made the competition seem more legit. I convinced myself I had just become the South Atlantic Surfing Champion. While no one other than Andy ever actually called me that, it did enhance my resume a good deal. I found out the next day that the locals really resented so many out of towners invading their beach. It was like that almost everywhere, as I learned early on in Galveston, but you just had to deal with it.

The next day Andy had already had a little sign printed up for the front window that said *Meet South Atlantic Surfing Champ Corky Sandoval Here*. Cheesy, but I guess I might have done the same thing if I owned the shop. I spent hours that day shaking hands and even signing a few autographs, but only for tourists. Most locals avoided me. I don't think I sold anything to a local that day, but I sold a ton of t-shirts.

Near closing a sort of surly looking guy, who might have been a little stoned, came into the shop and milled around for a while. Finally, he came up to me and asked if I was 'that Corky'. I felt a little cornered and decided the best answer was 'No, man. I'm this Corky'. That seemed to confuse him, and he wandered out.

"Do you know who that was?" Andy asked, walking up from the store room.

"Not a clue."

"That was Ken Phillips. They call him The Duke. He is used to winning almost every competition from here to Sebastian Inlet. I guess you got the better of him."

That explained a lot. I made a mental note to steer clear of The Duke. That proved to be not only difficult but unnecessary.

Andy and Gabe had gotten to know each other while watching me surf the competition and Andy seemed to love my buddy's Hawaiian vibe. Gabe ended up getting a shift at the shop as well, but he was on the morning watch before most tourists began the stroll on the strip. None-the-less, Gabe lived up the 'gift' and ended up with pretty good sales numbers in his first week. Andy was impressed.

After about a month and a half or so Abby, Gabe and I had a pretty good little nest egg, and Skipper was definitely getting a bit chubby. We took that as a sign that we should start talking about moving on. As it had been with Ben, we knew it would be really hard to tell Andy once we made our decision on the timing and destination. In reality, I'd grown really fond of Daytona Beach, if not the break. I might have been talked into staying if I was by myself I guess.

On the other hand, like some song said at the time, I was on a quest for the perfect wave.

Chapter Eight

THE DUKE OF CURL

That evening, we decided to wait a couple of days to tell Andy and only then when we had a definite destination. Our plan was to move on up the east coast getting local recommendations for the surf break as we went.

The next morning, I was out at seven o'clock to catch the early surf. Before I could snag my first ride, I saw The Duke walking down the beach towards me with his board under his arm. I was a bit apprehensive since he had seemed miffed when he visited the shop. I was surprised when he walked up and offered his hand for a shake. For some reason I assumed he would use the brother shake and again I got caught between one style and the other. We both laughed, both of us nervously.

"I'm Ken Phillips."

"I know, Andy told me. The Duke, right?"

"Just Duke, I guess. Kinda used to it," he replied. "I just wanted to apologize if I seemed pissed off or whatever yesterday. I guess I'm not used to losing. But I really dig your style and wanted you to know."

"I get it, man. I don't like outsiders out surfing me in California either. But we're cool," I said, hoping he was sincere.

"For you this must seem like kid's stuff compared to the big surf where you come from," Duke said.

"My feeling is you can find a ridable wave almost anywhere. Lots of surfers remind me that you just have to be patient."

"Good attitude, man. They say golf is frustrating, but surfing is a lot of hurry up and wait most days. At least on the East Coast."

"So, do you work around here somewhere?" I asked.

"Right now, I'm living with my folks in Ormond. My dad owns a furniture store and I help out there two or three days a week. But other than that, I'm just kind of chilling this summer," he responded. "So, what's your story?"

"My friends and I are just trying to see the country before maybe going back to school. The important word there is 'maybe'. I just haven't decided what I'm going to do but I'm going to surf as much as I can before I make that decision."

"I did a year of college at Florida State", Duke continued, "but bailed after that. My dad was not a happy dude, so I promised to go back sometime. But who knows."

"How 'bout the draft?", I asked carefully.

"4F"

"Same here."

Nuff said.

Duke and I decided to paddle out and see if we could pick up a ride or two. Of course, we ended up sitting on our boards comparing surfing stories. He was really stoked that I had done some surfing in Hawaii and asked a lot of questions about the break in certain areas. Finally, we were able to catch a wave or two. We managed to surf more or less side by side for a short period of time and I was impressed that Duke could walk the board with ease. He told me he was a longboard guy and couldn't really understand the shortboard phenomenon. He also agreed with Andy that the right to left aspect of Daytona Beach favored the longboard. I also felt it was best for a goofy foot. It just felt more comfortable.

Frankly, I wasn't clear how I had managed to beat this local top surfer, but at least I had met a kindred spirit.

Reasonably satisfied with our rides, we pulled our boards out of the water and began to head for the boardwalk.

"So, what's your plan, Corky, are you going to hang around here for a while?" Duke asked.

"Don't tell Andy but we plan on heading out in a couple of weeks. Don't know yet where we might end up. Any ideas?"

"Well, if you haven't surfed First Peak down at Sebastian Inlet, you probably should consider that. It's a much bigger break."

"Funny, that's the second time someone has mentioned Sebastian Inlet in the past couple of days.", I replied, "Where is it?"

"'Bout a hundred or so miles south of here. You think the locals here are touchy. Down there they might just run you off the beach."

"So, I might not even get to put my board in?"

"Well maybe I can tag along. They may not like seeing a goofy foot from California, but they know me, and I think they'd leave you alone if they think we are friends."

"So, are you willing to head down there for a few days with us?"

"Sure.", Duke said finally planting his board in the sand.

"In that case we're friends." I laughed. "But seriously, we were planning to head north up the coast. I really should check with my crew. Should be cool though." Duke and I turned to face the ocean and he seemed a bit reflective.

"Speaking of your crew, what's the deal with your red headed friend. Is she your girlfriend?"

"Nah. Just a pal. I thought about it, but she wasn't interested. Why?"

"Just really cute, that's all. Didn't want to move in on your action.", Duke assured me.

"I don't think you should count on much action. She's a sweet girl. I mean *sweet*. Vegetarian. Doesn't drink except for a beer about once a month. You know."

"Sure. Just curious. I haven't even spoken to her. No expectations. The guy traveling with you. He looks Asian or something. What's his story?"

"Oh, his name is Kaapo but we call him Gabe. He's a really good dude, just a little lazy sometimes. We've known each other since high school back in Hawaii."

"Ah, Hawaiian. Quite a crew!"

"And Skipper, too," I said, unintentionally making a pretty tacky rhyme.

Later that day, I talked to Gabe and Abby about the prospect of heading south and having at least a temporary traveling companion. As expected, Gabe was down with it, but Abby didn't seem all that enthused.

"I'm eager to see New England," she said. "How long do you think we'll be down there?"

"Couple of days, max, Abby," I pulled out of the air. "Just want to surf a really good break."

She finally agreed, and we discussed when we would tell our employers and how. Abby didn't think her boss would have much trouble finding another waitress, but Gabe and I had become a draw for Jack's. Me because of the championship and Gabe just because he was Hawaiian. Andy said sales were up a lot. He wasn't going to be too happy. We decided to give a two week notice and head south after that.

As expected, Andy was disappointed, but he didn't blow a gasket. He did try to convince us to stay, but we explained our goal and he finally accepted the inevitable. After all, in the mid 60s, lots of kids moved around a lot and some of them were actually his customers. In any case, I was going to miss this guy. He was a great boss and a good dude.

Two weeks passed quickly and the day before we were to head out, Andy asked us to lunch. I suggested inviting Duke and Andy agreed right away. We decided to have lunch at the bar where Abby had been working. It was really close, and we had all gotten to know the owner Leslie. In fact, Abby and Leslie had become pretty good friends while we were there.

"You guys have been a real blast to know," Andy said. "I don't want to keep trying to get you to change your mind, but I do want to suggest that you consider coming back and making this home."

"You know I'll be back," Duke said. "In fact, I'll be back after we head down to First Peak for a little side trip."

"Sure Duke, I know you will," Andy said. He didn't sound convinced.

We enjoyed a nice lunch. Of course, Abby knew the menu pretty well and easily found veggie foods to her liking. Wouldn't have mattered really. Leslie would have made her anything she wanted. Seeing the sadness in Leslie's eyes, I started to feel a little sad myself. But you had to pursue your own dreams I guess.

"You know, Andy, I'm still wondering where the name Jack's came from," I said. I hadn't really thought much about it since I began working at the surf shop but Andy's original response of 'you got me there' still stuck with me.

"Okay, here's the deal. Jack was my dad. He opened a sailing shop here in the early fifties. Catered to sailors and stink boat captains mostly. He put all his money into making it a success and really wanted me to help him. I fought him for a while and finally gave in and came to work as a stock boy and finally front room salesman. When he got sick in '62, I took over as manager on what I thought was a temporary basis. Unfortunately, that wasn't the case. He died in '63 and left the store to me. When surfing became a big deal, I changed the shop name slightly but wanted to keep the name Jack out front. So that's it. The whole story.", Andy explained, exhaling as if he'd revealed a well-kept secret.

"And here you are with a successful surf shop," I said.

"Well, here I am with a surf shop anyway."

Duke looked like he was holding back something and finally chimed in.

"Andy, everyone on Daytona Beach thinks you're the man. The daddy of surfing here in this darned tourist trap. We all feel welcome here. You did that for us. We won't forget that."

I actually thought I saw a little tear in Duke's eye, but I'm sure I was mistaken.

The next day we were preparing to leave when we had to deal with a little dilemma. Duke had a longboard a lot like mine and we had to transport both boards to Sebastian. Andy came to the rescue with a rig that stacked and secured the boards on the top of our car.

"What do we owe you, boss?" I asked.

"Not a dime, Corky. Just keep us in mind when you head back north. I could use a good assistant manager."

Leslie from the bar had hiked over to Jack's to say goodbye and after hugs all around we headed directly to the A1A for a little unplanned side trip. A1A is much like the Pacific Coast Highway on the west coast in that you catch some pretty cool shots of the ocean from time to time since it follows the coast.

Gabe had been demoted from shotgun to the back seat with Abby and Skip only because Duke was our guide. But Gabe pouted a while anyway.

As we drove I heard an occasional click. Glancing back, I noticed that Gabe had a little camera and was snapping shots of the ocean when a view presented itself.

"Hey, bro, I didn't even know you had a camera," I said.

"I picked this up second hand back in Galveston. You just aren't too observant. If you were, you'd have noticed that I've been taking pictures since then. Don't know when I'll ever have enough money to develop them though."

"Well if you think they're any good we'll figure out a way to make that happen," Abby piped up.

"So, Duke, we have a matched set here. A writer and a photographer. Could be a match made in heaven," I said, laughing.

"You can laugh now but who knows. Gabe might someday be a famous photographer," Abby replied.

"From your lips to God's ear," Gabe said

"Jeez, man, where did you come up with that little saying?" I said, laughing again.

"Just something my dad used to say. I guess you don't remember but I actually took a photography class back in high school."

"Sorry, man. I guess I was surfing at the time."

We continued our drive, just talking occasionally about the little oceanfront neighborhoods we encountered along the way. Duke told me a guy with a little bit of money could retire anywhere along A1A and live pretty well. I knew that wasn't the case along the oceanfront on the Pacific coast.

"Corky, I just remembered there is a fairly important competition at Sebastian Inlet in about a week," Duke said. "Wow! How could I have forgotten?" Somehow, I think Duke was well aware of the event.

"Hey, wait a minute," Abby jumped in. "I thought we'd only be here a couple of days."

"Don't jump to conclusions, Abby, we don't even know if I can enter the thing."

"Let me worry about that," Gabe stated. "After all, I'm your manager".

Hadn't heard that for a while.

"It's called the Inlet Challenge. Truth is this a good purse for the winner. A grand or so I think," Duke continued, taking all of us by surprise since that sort of money was unheard of at the time, "That's the good news. The bad news is it costs seventy-five bucks just to enter."

"You still going to handle that, Gabe?" I asked.

"I got this," Gabe responded, snapping another picture.

"Duke, we need to find a way for us both to compete. That increases our odds of coming away with money by double," I suggested.

"Agree, if they let us in," Duke reminded us.

"I got this," Gabe said again.

And he did have it.

Chapter Nine

PEAK PERFORMANCE

Turns out Sebastian Inlet was in a state park not too far from Vero Beach. It was beautiful country and my anticipation started to grow as we approached what they called First Peak. We had to walk a bit before having our first look at the phenom, but it was worth the effort. I hadn't imagined a break this big on the east coast based on what I'd heard and read.

There were several surfers out and Duke told me it was a fairly average showing for this spot. Mostly locals, he reminded me. I asked him if we should head back to the car for our boards, but he let me know pretty quickly that there were some steps to follow before moving from tourist on the beach to competitor, or even casual surfer.

So, we resigned ourselves to sitting on the beach and watching the action. The ocean was really blue that day, unlike most days on the Atlantic side I had learned. This looked more like a beach in Cali, so I felt right at home. Must have been the brilliant blue of the sky I figured.

Abby was clearly bored, and Gabe settled down for a good snooze, but Duke and I watched attentively. My new surfing pal pointed out a couple of the best guys and we paid particular attention to them, although everybody out that day seemed pretty good.

"That's Kelly over there," Duke said. "He's a grom but everyone is pretty stoked about his skill."

"Wait a minute, is that the same Kelly I met up in Pensacola?" I asked.

"Doubt it. This dude is only thirteen."

I was blown away by what I saw and wasn't at all sure I could compete at the Peak. But if Gabe could pull off getting us in, I was determined to give it a go. That day around noon I had my answer about Gabe's skill as my manager. He flagged me down while Duke and I were trying to scope waves and handed both of us a registration form.

"How did you pull this off, man?" I asked. I was amazed.

"Gift of Gabe," he said. "Anyway, I had a couple of hundred more on me after Las Vegas. Saved it for a rainy day. You're in. They really wanted the registration money."

"So much for the locals ruling," Duke said. "Your buddy is amazing, Corky." He shook Gabe's hand. "I owe ya dude."

"Yep, you do," Gabe responded.

So, we were in. The actual competition was the next weekend. Duke and I spent our time practicing on the wedge at First Peak. As Duke had predicted, the locals didn't give us much trouble since he was pretty well known at Sebastian Inlet.

Of course, Abby didn't show much interest in our preparations. She took the Buggy and headed over to the beach towns looking for arts and crafts I guess. She also found some restaurants not too far away. She insisted we try them at least. It was a small price to pay for her patience. I finally got used to corn on the cob. And one place introduced us all to grits. At first, I had no idea what they were, but I learned.

Thanks to Andy and Leslie, we finally had enough money to stay in a pretty nice place in Vero Beach about twelve miles away. The three guys camped out in one room and Abby and Skip had another. Not adjoining but on the same floor.

Being a real trouper, Skipper had become a source of constant amusement. He'd bonded with all of us, but particularly Abby, of course. I guess she was 'mommy' to our little pal. Maybe I was 'poppy', but it could have been either Gabe or me. No matter, he was one of the crew and we really enjoyed having him along. Of course, Abby did the heavy lifting of feeding and walking him, but she didn't seem to mind.

Duke and I were in high anticipation if not anxiety about the coming competition. The Inlet Challenge was a big deal in this part of Florida and even some places on the East Coast. Duke gave me some pointers, having surfed Sebastian Inlet a few of times before. But he said it could be pretty unpredictable and I shouldn't bet the farm that the break would behave in any particular way. Not that any could be relied upon from Hawaii to Africa to Orange County, to this part of the country. So, all you could do is sit, watch and play the odds.

Finally, the day of the competition arrived and my confidence had improved. Duke said his had too. While the locals were used to us by now, it was part of their routine to harass the newbies to First Peak and we took our share of ribbing. We decided to take it in stride since to react or push back would break our concentration and egg them on to even more mouthy behavior.

The field of surfers that day was a cross section of humanity. Some oldies, some groms, some buff surf dudes and, well, us. Quite frankly, we were none of the above (except 'us' of course). I'm not sure that scanning the competition boosted my confidence or just confused the situation but I was determined to make a good showing. Duke and I had agreed to take this whole thing seriously.

A horn blew and like in Daytona, we all gathered at a central spot to hear the very obvious rules read out. Blah, blah, blah. Once that was done and the numbers assigned and pinned to our shirts or sometimes our baggies (what a crock), we all prepared to head out.

I loved days like this for surfing and particularly competing. It was sunny and warm with a breeze coming southeast to northwest. Perfect I thought.

The break was equally spectacular that day and I had to admit I hadn't seen this big a surf since leaving California. I was a bit intimidated but decided to try for the best finish I could muster.

When I caught my first wave, I knew I was in my groove. The ride was almost automatic. I walked the board almost at will and managed to finish standing on the beach. A couple of times I faltered but never did get dumped. Occasionally, I would glance over at Duke. He was having a good day as well and all of a sudden, I realized he was my biggest competition. I was determined to best my new buddy, but he hung in there, ride after ride. This guy was no beginner. I had a lot of respect for both his style and focus. Damned good surfer.

As we got to the final competition we knew we were neck in neck. I don't think that mattered at all. We were just happy it was the two of us and not some hotshot local with an ax to grind.

My last wave was a work of art. It crested at what I thought was easily four feet above my head, curled perfectly and formed an impressive barrel. It was all I could do not to allow my excitement to overcome my concentration. I had to come out of the barrel in prime position to ride the wave on into the beach and end my ride standing up.

I was elated when I emerged and could tell I had a clean ride to the beach. I didn't know if my ride was a winner, but I knew it was one of the best waves and rides of my life. As I walked out of the surf Gabe was running up to me.

"You got this Corky," he was almost yelling. "Even the judges were saying 'wow'. I'm telling you, you got this."

I saw Duke not too far away and headed down to ask him about his last wave. He hadn't caught the same one I had I gathered but the ocean was spitting out some pretty good stuff at that point.

"How was your ride, Duke?"

"Not as good as yours but I think I might have a chance." Duke was beaming.

We all milled around for a while waiting for the organizers to call everyone together for the announcement of the winners. Even though my last ride was my best, maybe ever, I was still not convinced it was possible for a California guy to win here. I assumed even the judges would be a little prejudiced against outsiders. I guess I didn't need to worry.

When the announcement of the winners was made I was stunned. I had won. Duke was second. Two boys from out of the area had taken top honors. Duke didn't seem at all disappointed that I had beaten him. In fact, he ran up to me and hugged me like the brother he was becoming.

Both Duke and I won small trophies but more importantly there was the money. As Duke had told me, I won two hundred and fifty dollars and he raked in one hundred for second. Our team was finally in the money. At that point it really did seem like a team. Gabe was pulling strings to get us the opportunity to compete and Duke and I were working hard to make it worth our while. I didn't realize until later that even Abby would factor into the surfing aspect of our trip, or at least the story of the trip. She was a lady of surprises.

A celebration was in order of course. Even Abby was eager to spend an evening acknowledging our wins. Gabe had found a sports bar nearby that seemed to have a pretty good menu, so we all headed over there. I knew the three guys would hoist more than a few beers. Heck maybe Abby might even join us for one or two. She did, and it turned out that she could be really funny once she got into the spirit of things.

"So, do we hang out here for a while or move on up the coast?" Duke asked after dinner.

"Gee, Duke, I wasn't sure you would want to come along, but it would be a gas if you did," I told him

"I'm in, man. This is good fun and I don't have anything holding me back right now."

"Abby. I think you should weigh in on this since you've been so understanding." I said.

"Well I'm eager to see more of the east coast. But I'm good taking our time. Where can we go from here that gives you guys a chance to surf and me a chance to explore? I'd like to write some more about our trip and I think the south is such a cool subject."

I wasn't certain if Abby was being totally sincere or just agreeable. I was growing more fond of her and really noticed and appreciated her maturity. God knows all of us guys had to rely on it.

"Maybe we should head up to the Carolinas. I've heard that there are spots there with reasonable breaks," Gabe suggested. "I think there is even a competition at Folly Beach near Charleston that might be worth heading for if you guys are up for it."

Skipper didn't object.

"Sounds like a winner to me," I said, "Let's head out in a couple of days and just work slowly up the coast," I suggested.

I knew Abby would enjoy a few stops along the way to add to her journal, and Gabe was getting pretty serious about his photography, even though we hadn't had the opportunity to see any of his photos yet. I made a mental note to encourage him to get some developed when we arrived in Charleston. After all, he was partly responsible for our winnings.

We decided to stay as close to the water as we could as we headed north, so we could keep an eye out for a reasonable break and to enjoy the scenery and seafood. While we drove through Florida, we knew we would stay close to A1A but weren't sure about sticking with Highway 1 once we left the state. It turned out that to achieve our goal of remaining close to the ocean, we needed to take some side trips and head east, at least on the first leg of our trip north.

A lifeguard in Daytona had mentioned a place called Hilton Head Island on the south coast of South Carolina, not far from Savannah, Georgia. He said he'd heard there were some cool things going on there but didn't know anything about the surf. We were all just curious to explore some new oceanfront territory so decided to make Hilton Head our first side trip. Duke was still riding shotgun and did his best to manage the roadmaps and keep us moving. He did a nice job except for getting the maps folded back up. He got pretty frustrated but the rest of us had a good laugh.

Once we worked our way over to Hilton Head Island, we quickly found a place to stay at the Port Royal Inn on the north end. They were a traditional resort style motel but also had villas. We had a little money from our winnings and decided to splurge and rent a villa for a couple of days so that we wouldn't have to hide Skipper.

The island is about fourteen miles long and we never could find out how wide. It was not your typical tourist trap but more like a nice coastal neighborhood. We decided to take some time to explore and get to know the place. I was blown away by some of the beaches, particularly a place called Dolphin Head. Some people called it "Ghost Beach" because an early property owner had drowned just off the coast. I felt some sort of sensation as we looked out over the water, but even today I don't understand what I was feeling.

We obviously asked around about a surf break, but the closest we got was meeting a few guys from something called the Hunting Island Surf Club. It seemed like they spent their time moving from place to place in what they called 'the Lowcountry' looking for a place to put in a board. The rest of the time was spent hanging around complaining about not finding one. They did back up the claims that Folly Beach up by Charleston could provide a good ride when conditions were favorable. So, we were on the right track.

One afternoon everyone had different goals and I was sitting alone at a little funky beachfront bar. The bartender, who for some reason called himself 'Chicken Jack', was chatty and full of information about the island and South Carolina in general. He had the radio tuned to a station in nearby Savannah that seemed to specialize in Beachboys music along with some Jan and Dean and other surf music. I felt right at home.

I felt a sense of well being sitting there looking at a very beautiful beach, but really modest surf. I don't think I had ever felt that before. Break or no break, for some reason I just knew I'd be back to this special place.

And now for a little historical perspective:

Billboard magazine's Top Hot 100 songs of 1966.[1]

No	Title	Artist(s)
1	"Ballad of the Green Berets"	SSgt. Barry Sadler
2	"Cherish"	The Association
3	"(You're My) Soul and Inspiration"	The Righteous Brothers
4	"Reach Out I'll Be There"	Four Tops
5	"96 Tears"	? and the Mysterians
6	"Last Train to Clarksville"	The Monkees
7	"Monday, Monday"	The Mamas & the Papas
8	"You Can't Hurry Love"	The Supremes
9	"Poor Side of Town"	Johnny Rivers
10	"California Dreamin'"	The Mamas & the Papas
11	"Summer In The City"	The Lovin' Spoonful
12	"Born Free"	Roger Williams
13	"These Boots Are Made for Walkin'"	Nancy Sinatra
14	"What Becomes of the Brokenhearted"	Jimmy Ruffin
15	"Strangers in the Night"	Frank Sinatra
16	"We Can Work It Out"	The Beatles
17	"Good Lovin'"	The Young Rascals
18	"Winchester Cathedral"	The New Vaudeville Band
19	"Hanky Panky"	Tommy James and the Shondells
20	"When a Man Loves a Woman"	Percy Sledge
21	"Paint It, Black"	The Rolling Stones
22	"My Love"	Petula Clark
23	"Lightnin' Strikes"	Lou Christie
24	"Wild Thing"	The Troggs
25	"Kicks"	Paul Revere & the Raiders
26	"Sunshine Superman"	Donovan
27	"Sunny"	Bobby Hebb
28	"Paperback Writer"	The Beatles
29	"See You In September"	The Happenings
30	"You Keep Me Hangin' On"	The Supremes
31	"Li'l Red Riding Hood"	Sam the Sham and the Pharaohs
32	"Molly"	Mitch Ryder & the Detroit Wheels
33	"Good Vibrations"	The Beach Boys
34	"A Groovy Kind of Love"	The Mindbenders
35	"You Don't Have To Say You Love Me"	Dusty Springfield
36	"Cool Jerk"	The Capitols
37	"Born a Woman"	Sandy Posey
38	"Red Rubber Ball"	The Cyrkle
39	"B-A-B-Y"	Carla Thomas
40	"Walk Away Renée"	The Left Banke
41	"Daydream"	The Lovin' Spoonful
42	"Time Won't Let Me"	The Outsiders
43	"Hooray for Hazel"	Tommy Roe
44	"Sweet Pea"	Tommy Roe
45	"Bus Stop"	The Hollies
46	"I'm Your Puppet"	James & Bobby Purify
47	"I'm So Lonesome I Could Cry"	B. J. Thomas
48	"Ain't Too Proud to Beg"	The Temptations
49	"Dirty Water"	The Standells
50	"Elusive Butterfly"	Bob Lind

51	"I Am a Rock"	Simon & Garfunkel
52	"Crying Time"	Ray Charles
53	"Secret Agent Man"	Johnny Rivers
54	"The Sound of Silence"	Simon & Garfunkel
55	"Lady Godiva"	Peter and Gordon
56	"Homeward Bound"	Simon & Garfunkel
57	"Did You Ever Have to Make Up Your Mind?"	The Lovin' Spoonful
58	"Barefootin'"	Robert Parker
59	"Uptight (Everything's Alright)"	Stevie Wonder
60	"Bang Bang (My Baby Shot Me Down)"	Cher
61	"Sloop John B"	The Beach Boys
62	"19th Nervous Breakdown"	The Rolling Stones
63	"Wipe Out"	The Surfaris
64	"Psychotic Reaction"	Count Five
65	"Beauty Is Only Skin Deep"	The Temptations
66	"No Matter What Shape (Your Stomach's In)"	The T-Bones
67	"Just Like Me"	Paul Revere & the Raiders
68	"Love Makes the World Go Round"	Deon Jackson
69	"The Pied Piper"	Crispian St. Peters
70	"Coming On Strong"	Brenda Lee
71	"Somewhere My Love"	Ray Conniff Singers
72	"Almost Persuaded"	David Houston
73	"If I Were a Carpenter"	Bobby Darin
74	"Don't Mess with Bill"	The Marvelettes
75	"Cherry, Cherry"	Neil Diamond
76	"Working In The Coal Mine"	Lee Dorsey
77	"Message to Michael"	Dionne Warwick
78	"Love Is a Hurtin' Thing"	Lou Rawls
79	"Barbara Ann"	The Beach Boys
80	"Gloria"	The Shadows of Knight
81	"My World Is Empty Without You"	The Supremes
82	"Rainy Day Women #12 & 35"	Bob Dylan
83	"Guantanamera"	The Sandpipers
84	"Land of 1000 Dances"	Wilson Pickett
85	"Oh How Happy"	The Shades of Blue
86	"Woman"	Peter and Gordon
87	"You Baby"	The Turtles
88	"Five O'Clock World"	The Vogues
89	"Black Is Black"	Los Bravos
90	"Nowhere Man"	The Beatles
91	"Dandy"	Herman's Hermits
92	"Baby Scratch My Back"	Slim Harpo
93	"She's Just My Style"	Gary Lewis & The Playboys
94	"The More I See You"	Chris Montez
95	"I Fought the Law"	Bobby Fuller Four
96	"Yellow Submarine"	The Beatles
97	"Hungry"	Paul Revere & the Raiders
98	"Zorba the Greek"	Herb Alpert and the Tijuana Brass
99	"Shapes of Things"	The Yardbirds
100	"634-5789 (Soulsville, U.S.A.)"	Wilson Picket

[1] From Wikipedia, the free encyclopedia

Chapter Ten

FUN AND FOLLY

After a couple of restful days on the island, we headed back out to the highway and charted our course northward. Gabe had negotiated his way back to shotgun. Don't really know how, but he was my original navigator, so it was fine with me. He was also better at refolding maps.

We came to find out that following Highway 17 up the coast was a better option than Highway 1. That coastal route allowed us to have a look at some little towns along our route. You could tell there was something in the air and that tourists were starting to discover this part of the east coast as an alternative to driving much further south to vacation in Florida. That seemed to be the normal destination for obvious reasons, but things were happening here. In fact, later in our trip I thought Myrtle Beach reminded me of our time in Daytona. Something was popping.

I was kind of surprised that the people in the area were welcoming of some California and Florida kids with surf boards on the top of their car. But maybe we were living at a time when accepting other lifestyles was becoming more common. Then again, maybe not.

It took us a little over three hours to get to the Charleston area from Hilton Head. It was a beautiful day to drive and the whole team was in an upbeat mood. When we arrived, we had to ask around for a good while before we got directions to Folly Beach and the pier and pavilion area we were told to find. Folly Beach turned out to be one big carnival. There was a dance pavilion, an amusement park and you could hear music coming out of somewhere, presumably a bar, even though it was only about two in the afternoon.

We found a parking place near the beach and, leaving the boards behind for the moment, ventured down to the waterfront to check out the break. Even though the wind seemed fairly calm, we were pretty impressed with the size of the waves and the number of surfers out that day. Duke pointed out that there were even some girls catching waves. A couple of them were really good and would give any guy a run for his money in a competition. I made another of my mental notes to try to meet one and get her story.

"No sense just hanging around here," Duke said, "Let's go get the boards."

Gabe and Abby decided to scout a bit and maybe grab a hotdog, but Duke and I were eager to hit the water and that overpowered our hunger. It was about eighty-five degrees and sunny. There was a light breeze. It was a classic day for surfing and we weren't about to waste it.

No sooner had we paddled out when we saw a really large swell further out and just had a hunch it would break so that we could catch a ride. Sure enough, Duke and I were both able to grab that first one and ride it all the way into the beach. It sure felt good to be off the road again and back in the water. We were both laughing at our good fortune when we paddled back out. We caught some more pretty good waves that day, but none were as exciting as the first one.

After being in the water for about an hour and a half, we were sitting on our boards waiting for some action when I noticed one of the girl surfers sitting on her board and watching the swells intently. I may not have been paying enough attention, but I didn't recall having seen too many girls surfing in most of the locations we visited on the east coast.

I couldn't help but stare at the girl. She was really cute. Dark hair slicked straight back, perfect tan and really tiny. I don't think she could have been much over five feet tall if that. She finally noticed me looking her way and I found I was pretty embarrassed to be caught. She smiled for a second but then turned her attention back to the water and another promising swell heading our way.

The girl caught the break perfectly and expertly rode the wave all the way in. As for me. I was too distracted, and the wave broke over my head before I could react. I popped back up coughing and trying to hang onto my board. I could hear the girl laughing even over the roar of the ocean. *Some Corktop*, I thought to myself.

She paddled back out in my direction still chuckling.

"Good form," she said. "Even for a grom."

"Well it's your fault," I replied, knowing she would immediately know what I meant, "but I'm definitely not a grom."

"Whatever you say," she said.

I felt a little courage building back and extended my hand.

"I'm Corky Sandoval from California," I said, hoping to impress her.

"Well hello, Corky, I'm Alexa De Silva, *not* from California."

She was not impressed. However, she did shake my hand.

"What are doing in South Carolina…umm…Corky?"

"I know it doesn't look like it, but I'm trying to do some surfing. I heard there was a competition here."

"I heard that too, but their big event was in January."

"Wow! Had to be pretty cold here."

I remounted my board and we both turned around to face the break.

"Where are you from really," I said trying to maintain my concentration.

"Rhode Island, actually, near Newport."

"Is there a break there?"

"Come on, California, haven't you ever heard of Ruggles?", Alexa seemed incredulous.

"Don't think so, but I haven't surfed the east coast much."

"Major break right to left and you get some awesome barrels."

Instead of this girl being impressed, I was. She knew her surfing and didn't mind showing her savvy, or her surfing skill.

"That's a perfect break for a goofy," I said.

"So I'm told." Based on the blank look on her face I think she was on the verge of paddling away.

"Do you surf competitively?" I asked, trying to save the day.

"There are a few competitions here and there specifically for females and it's like impossible to get into the guy's events. So, I don't get to really compete much. How 'bout you, have you won anything I might have heard of?"

"I won down at Sebastian Inlet just the other day in fact."

"Impressive," Alexa said, then finally found a wave she could ride.

I popped up as well and did a lot better than the last ridable wave. We were almost side by side most of the ride and ended up hitting the beach in sync. I had almost forgotten about Duke but found him sitting on the beach chatting up what turned out to be the second female surfer we'd seen.

Alexa and I walked up to Duke and the other girl.

"Duke, meet Alexa, one sweet surfer," I said, immediately realizing I chosen the wrong word. Alexa just looked at me with that *you should know better* look in her eyes. She was going to make someone a great wife.

"Alexa, this is my buddy, Duke."

They exchanged hellos and Duke introduced the other girl as Stacy, also from Rhode Island. Duke and Stacy seemed to be hitting it off and pretty soon the four of us were sitting cross legged and sharing stories of big breaks and awesome parties. Life was good.

Apparently, Gabe and Abby had seen us from the pavilion and joined us on the beach. Soon we realized that we needed to eat and find a place to crash. Stacy said she knew an awesome Italian restaurant and I admitted I'd been craving pizza for about a month, so we all headed out to lock down our boards and reconnect to have dinner. The pizza joint had an outdoor terrace and we asked nicely if Skipper could sit under the table, assuring the manager he wouldn't bother anyone. He was cool about it.

Later everyone had eaten way too much pizza and drank too much beer, we realized we still had no place to stay. Alexa piped up and said she and Stacy had rented a little apartment for the summer and since it was getting later we could crash there, but just for one night. I'm sure she wouldn't have offered that if Abby hadn't been with us but all of us were grateful.

After the group watched some TV and got to know each other a little better, Abby was able to sleep on a nice couch in the living room and the guys sacked out on the floor. It had been a good day and I had met a girl that I thought might figure into my future, if she could just stop laughing at me. That thought made *me* chuckle.

The next morning, we woke up to the smell of bacon. Stacey had gotten up early and gone to the supermarket to buy a large quantity of eggs and bacon along with a couple of potatoes to fry. I don't think I'd ever woken up to a more heavenly smell.

Our entire group pigged out, that is except Abby of course. Alexa and Stacy had no idea Abby was a vegetarian but managed to find provide a nice bowl of cereal and toast with jelly. Abby was happy with that, although I thought I noticed her at least appreciating the smell of the bacon.

After breakfast, we had a little informal meeting and discussed how we might spend the day. The four surfers didn't hesitate to state a preference for heading back to the beach. Abby and Gabe volunteered to search for a motel where we could rent a couple of rooms. Alexa said we could stay another night if we liked, but Abby didn't want to inconvenience them any more than we had, and Abby was surf mommy by this point.

Duke told the girls that we'd hoped to find a competition. Alexa said there were only some unofficial events held on weekends. Most just offered prizes like gift certificates or occasionally cheesy trophies. We didn't realize it, but Gabe had been at work and found a group called the West Coast East Surf Club that had planned a more formal meet about a week later. Darned if he hadn't become a really good team manager. We hadn't necessarily planned on staying that long, but now we had more than one reason to do so. I wanted to get to know Alexa and it seemed like Duke felt the same about Stacy.

So, we settled in to our day to day life on Folly Beach, surfing during the day and getting to know each other each evening. Alexa had let down her guard a bit and I'd have to say we'd become friends, even though I hoped for more.

The Surf Club consisted of several guys from the area who were top notch surfers with a great feel for the break at Folly. The competition they were holding was on a Saturday. Typically, when they sponsored something they invited all comers to challenge them, mainly I guessed to show off a bit. They pooled their money and got a minor sponsorship from McKevlin's Surf Shop and offered a five-hundred-dollar prize. Generally, they were confident the prize would stay with the club and usually it did.

When Gabe put in our applications, he conveniently forgot to mention we were from the West Coast but he did reference points south. He also failed to mention our win at Sebastian Inlet. Those lost details must have given them the perception we were out of town east coast amateurs and probably no real threat. Clever boy that Gabe.

Gabe even tried to get the girls registered, but that didn't happen. The guys in the club didn't want to run the risk of losing to a girl I guess, particularly if they had seen Alexa and Stacy surf. First failure for the gift of Gabe.

Having surfed the Folly break for several days, I was pretty confident about a good showing. So was Duke. That Saturday was a nearly perfect day to surf. Because of a weather front off the coast there was a pretty good wind, although the skies were sunny. As a result, the waves were breaking further out and cresting into nice barrels from time to time. My kind of conditions.

Fortunately, or unfortunately, Duke and I were competing in different four-man heats. In my first twenty-minute set, I was able to catch two really smokin' waves and enjoyed a great score. Duke didn't do as well in his first ride, getting up nicely on a perfect crest but wiping out when the barrel started to form. It just didn't turn out to be his day, but I kept turning in good scores and, you guessed it, won that challenge rather easily. I could see that several of the boys from the club were not too happy about that, but a couple came up and congratulated me. Of course, they tried to pump me for information about my background, but I was able to dodge the questions successfully.

After I collected my not so bad winnings, we thought it might be a good idea to head somewhere for a late lunch or early dinner and talk about next steps. Alexa and Stacy were committed to staying put and riding out the summer months but planned to move on south for the winter. I found out that Stacy came from 'old money' and that her folks were staking her for a few months before she headed back to school. That turned out to be a common theme among the surf crowd we met that year.

I knew Duke was disappointed to move on before getting to really know Stacy, but he was committed to our journey and agreed. I did notice they kissed goodbye that last evening. Before we left, we agreed to try to catch up in south Florida as the winter set in and maybe share rent on a house. Since we had no way of reaching each other we convinced the girls to head to Daytona, find Jack's and ask Andy for a recommendation on where to look for a house. It figured that Andy would be pretty happy to find out his 'Cali Team' was coming back for the season. That decision perked Duke up a good bit.

The next day we broke camp and headed for Virginia Beach. Once again, Gabe kept his ear to the ground and found out there was a growing surf community there.

It was August 1967. The journey had just begun.

Chapter Eleven

THE EAST COAST SURFING CHAMPIONSHIP

Sunny day. 87 degrees and humid. Virginia Beach, Virginia.

I was pretty surprised at the number of tourists soaking up the sun in this coastal town. I can't say I was even aware of Virginia Beach growing up and hadn't heard much about it while traveling in the east. But here we were in what they called 'The Old Dominion' walking on flat white sand, stepping over hundreds of sunbathers, dodging footballs and Frisbees and trying hard to find anywhere you might put in a board. To me, the Atlantic looked like a big pond. Kids walked out for what looked like thirty yards before the water was waist deep. Kind of disappointing, and I thought the Gulf was glassy.

We decided there was no sense continuing to look for a break on this particular day and began looking for a place to stay. We agreed to try to check into a beachfront motel so that we could at least have a view. Might not get to surf but at a minimum we could feel at home on the water. We found a motel situated on the north end of the beach called The Colonial Inn that lived up to its name. Red brick. White railings. But it had views up and down the beach that rivaled anything on the Pacific coast, even if the waves were kid sized.

We had to hide Skipper since it was a 'no pets allowed' motel but he was a pretty quiet pup. Only real problem came when he needed to go outside to do his business. But we found back stairs and took turns sneaking him in and out.

It didn't take us long asking locals about surf break to find out we were on the wrong end of the beach. The only real consistent break was at an area reserved for surfing near the Virginia Beach fishing pier. We also found out there was actually a competition called The East Coast Surfing Championships happening that very month, although no one seemed to know the exact dates.

We decided to head to the surfing area the next morning. Not realizing how long the beach was we decided to walk. Duke and I were carrying our boards of course. Abby had stayed behind to write on the little ocean front deck at the hotel and to look after Skipper, but Gabe was with us. By the time we got to the steel pier as they called it, the ocean had kicked up a bit compared to the day before and several surfers were sitting on their boards in anticipation.

"I can't imagine there is a serious competition here," Duke said, surveying the surroundings in both directions.

"I think you're a surfing snob," I chuckled.

"Well a guy at the motel said the championship here is a pretty big deal for East Coast surfers," Gabe responded.

"Even some guys from the West Coast come over here sometimes."

"I guess we'll just have to see. But if it doesn't get any better than this we should talk about moving on," I suggested.

We hung around watching the action for a while before thinking about giving it a try. I noticed we were drawing some attention from the tourists and other surfers, maybe due to our dinged-up longboards or maybe because by this time we looked pretty scruffy. Plus, we were two tall thin white guys with dark tans and one Hawaiian dude built like a tank. Must have been a site. Most of the surfers we saw looked pretty college prep to us.

We were kind of surprised to find people managing to actually get up on their boards. Some were catching an occasional decent break and took advantage of even those cresting at three or four feet. We also noticed kids nearby skimming along the water's edge on round boards that looked like they were made of plywood. It was impressive that they could throw the board out in front of them, jump on and ride the board for a good way before jumping off or falling on their butts into the wet sand.

One kid who looked to be about twelve told us what they were riding were called 'piper boards'. I don't know where he got that, but I was only familiar with a round nosed single fin board used by surfers in Hawaii that had that name. I suspected somebody claimed the name for these rudimentary little round boards to help sell them to the kids. Either that or the kid we talked to was just goofy in a different way. No matter. Looked like fun and we agreed to try skimming before moving on.

Gabe saw a sign mentioning the championship and walked on to see if it had promise for us. He came running back to tell us we could still register. Even though the surf was unimpressive we decided to give it a go.

"There's another guy here named Corky," Gabe said, panting from his short sprint.

"Nah, couldn't be," I said. After all, it really couldn't be Corky Carroll could it?

"Didn't get his last name but the guy at the registration desk was surprised there was another one."

The entry fee turned out to be twenty-five dollars but there really wasn't any prize money. We had to think about surfing in a competition where we were paying with no chance for a return but decided it was worth it for the experience.

As we walked up to the registration area, I noticed a group of people standing around one guy, all of them seeming to be pretty star struck.

"Damn, Duke, that *is* Corky Carroll over there," I said, hardly believing my eyes. I couldn't imagine a West Coast champion surfer would show up to compete in what looked like a pretty minor competition. I decided I wanted to find out why he was here.

Gabe took care of registering us and I decided to walk over to Corky and try to maintain my cool. After all, he had been one of my role models. He was at the top of his game and they said he actually made a living surfing, although it was hard to imagine how.

I finally worked my way up to and through the small crowd, swallowed hard and managed to speak.

"Hey, Corky. I'm Corky. Corky Sandoval," I said. I guess I thought he might think the coincidence was interesting if not funny.

Corky looked at me like I was a little loopy.

"So, how did you get that name?" he asked, seeming about to laugh at the joke. I'm sure he assumed I had copped it from him, but I laid out the corktop swimming explanation quickly and he seemed to accept it.

Lots of people wanted to talk to him since he was one of the more famous surfers if not the most famous surfer in the world, but he was gracious enough to spend a minute or two kidding around with me.

"So how did you end up here?" I finally asked the obvious question.

"Aww, I'm on tour promoting Endless Summer," he responded. "Have you seen the movie?"

"I tried to get in to see it, but the line was around the block."

"Well it's worth seeing and does a lot of good for the sport," Corky said.

We talked for minute more. Corky extended his hand, shook mine and said, "Good luck, Corky. Hope you do well." And that was it. What a nice guy.

The rest of the day I was still reeling from meeting Corky Carroll and once the surfing began, I think it actually hurt my performance. After all, this other weird Corky, that would be me, was competing with a world champion. I imagined that people expected me to tank and maybe that caused me to think I would tank too. I had to really concentrate to turn in a relatively good performance.

It was a multiple day event and when the dust, well actually the sea foam, settled, Corky Carroll had placed second and I was what I felt like was a distant fifth. Duke didn't do as well and wasn't in the top ten. That was surprising to me since he was really technically better than I was. I wondered if he had Stacy on his mind. I'd have to ask him.

After the competition, we had to decide what to do next, go further north or concede the summer and head back south. Abby wanted to keep going. Gabe was indifferent. Not sure why, but both Duke and I were convinced that we should head back to Florida and ride out the winter there.

I was really concerned about Abby traveling by herself, particularly when she told us she planned to hitchhike most of the way to New England. By now I felt like I was a big brother to her, even though we were close to the same age. Late that night after the others had turned in, I asked her to sit on the deck outside her room to talk about her plans. It was a clear night and the moonlight danced on the waves. It was really peaceful, and both Abby and I breathed in the ocean air more than once.

"Abby, I'm worried about you. I hoped you would stay with the team for a while. How come you want to keep going north?"

"I've never really talked about this, but my roots are up in New England.", she explained, "I wasn't born there of course but a lot of my family was, mostly around New Bedford. I just feel like I've got to visit there to understand my background."

"I get that, but traveling alone can be pretty dangerous."

"I won't be alone. I've got Skipper. You will let me keep him, won't you?"

"Of course, but he's just a little dude. What good does that do?"

"He's small but he's mighty." She laughed. "Look, Corky, I don't try to fool myself. I know there are creeps out there and I won't take any chances, but if I don't do this now I might never do it. Anyway, I'm a writer."

"I believe you really are.", I said hoping she gathered how much I supported her.

We sat quietly for a while and stared at the ocean. Soon something dawned on me.

"Abby, I can't believe it, but in all the time we've traveled together you never told me your last name."

"I really I didn't do that on purpose, but it just didn't seem that important I guess."

"So, what is it, if you don't mind me asking."

"It's Colter," she replied looking at me.

"Colter?" Lights began to come on in my mind. "Hey, isn't that Ben's name?"

"Yes, Ben's my uncle. He's the main reason I moved to Half Moon Bay. I love him to death and wanted to be part of his life. He was always the one who told me to follow my dreams and never be afraid to try new things."

"Now I see why he helped us so much."

This conversation caused me to wonder about other parts of Abby's life. I also thought back to a comment Abby made about Joey, the young boy we'd befriended in Galveston. She had obviously felt that his life in some way was similar to hers. I knew I should proceed with caution but really wanted to understand more about my friend.

"Abby, I really don't know much about your life growing up. Sometimes you seem a little sad. Is there something that happened that we haven't talked about that you can share?"

"Not really, Corky. I just wasn't very close to my parents and it sort of blew up in my face my second year of high school.", she replied, appearing to tear up." I left home and wandered around for a while. I really felt lost because my folks were pressuring me to do this and do that and didn't listen much to my ideas and dreams. I know it sounds like a normal thing that teenagers go through, but for me it hurt. So, I left."

"I'm sorry, Abby. Are you back with your folks?"

"Yes, thanks to Ben. He listened to me, seemed to really be interested in my future. He also taught me to surf.", she wiped tears from her eyes and her mood brightened somewhat.

"Surf? Abby, I had no idea you had any interest in surfing. Why didn't you tell me?"

"I didn't want you to ask me to surf with you. I just didn't take to it."

"Why? What happened?"

"Nothing to me," Abby replied, "but when he was in his twenties, Ben broke his back surfing the big break at Half Moon Bay. He'd been a champion before that, but he was in the hospital for months."

"And he still taught you to surf?"

"Not only that. He taught me that riding the waves calmed the soul and put everything in perspective."

"But you quit."

"Yeah, but only after I realized how completely it had wrecked his body. I loved Ben so much and respected his courage. But I just lost my nerve when he told me the whole story. Sometimes I wish I'd stuck with it, but he didn't push me. He understood. Anyway, my uncle finally convinced me to head back home and give my parents a chance, try to see their point of view. Things were better after that. At least I got to rejoin him after I graduated. He will always be my shining star."

"Good," was all I could say. I felt like I knew Abby a lot better and even understood why I liked her so much. At least she had the courage to try surfing. It wasn't for everyone and she was happy to tell the stories of the kids she met along the way, surfers or otherwise. And Ben had become a real hero to me, for many reasons. At least Abby and I shared that.

We sat for a while longer until Skipper decided he needed to pee. I volunteered to do walking duties and we split for the evening. As I walked the little pup, I realized where Abby was coming from. Ben followed his dreams and finally ended up right where he wanted to be. She wanted the same type of life, one where her mind could run free and she could follow her dreams without fear of constant criticism. I finally got it.

We got up the next morning and found a little place for breakfast. We were all in a great mood and, having talked to Abby, I felt better about her plans. She promised that she would stay in touch and rejoin us later. I made sure she had the address at Andy's shop and suggested we all reunite there around Christmas. I wasn't at all sure she would show up, but it was worth a shot. I think Duke was the most disappointed that she wasn't sticking with the team. Or maybe it was Skipper he would miss. After all, Abby was the puppy momma but we all shared a love of the little mutt.

Later in the day, we gathered up our stuff and got ready to head in our different directions. I noticed that it wasn't Abby that teared up, it was Gabe. We had become a real team and had bonded on a whole different level. It seemed odd that it had come to an end, or at least it felt like that for the moment. He was surprised and just a bit hurt that Abby wanted to leave us. It made me wonder if he had hoped for a relationship with Abby. I hadn't seen that before.

So now I felt like I was seeing Duke pine over Stacey and maybe Gabe over Abby. Me, I had enjoyed my time with Alexa but had no idea where that could go or if I even wanted it to go anywhere. In any case, if the two surfer girls were at Jack's when we got there, time would tell.

We all hugged Abby, said our goodbyes and the guys got into the Buggy. We were all quiet as we started our journey back south. Something just wasn't right and we all knew it. But we supported Abby's need to pursue her life her way. We only hoped our paths would cross again.

Onward.

Chapter Twelve

A FEW SURPRISES

We decided to take it really slowly heading down the coast. We could still enjoy some surfing here and there and visit a few of the places we'd missed driving north. While we were in Virginia Beach, a guy from North Carolina told us to head over to Nags Head. We hadn't spent any time in North Carolina so decided that was a pretty good idea.

When we got to Nags Head and asked around about surfing spots, a few of the locals mentioned Jennette's Pier. They said the break was pretty reliable and most local surfers ended up there during the warmer months. The pier was actually one of the more impressive ones we had seen in our travels and the surf was significant but kind of choppy close in. Even so it was ridable and since we hadn't driven very long that day we decided to give it a try.

After a couple of good rides, we saw an unusually big set forming and faced up to be ready. As we rose up toward the initial crest, I caught it just perfectly but apparently Duke wasn't as lucky. I wasn't watching him of course but Gabe told me Duke left his board almost immediately and it came crashing down in what looked to Gabe like the very spot where Duke had gone under.

Once I finished my ride and turned back to face the ocean, I saw that Duke had surfaced but was bleeding from his forehead. It didn't look good. Every surfer knows you don't want to hang around in the water if you are bleeding so, being really experienced, Duke knew to get out of the water fast before any unwanted predators noticed the blood.

When he got to the beach, more or less dragging his board, Duke lay down holding his forehead and breathing heavily. There were lifeguards on duty and they ran up as quickly as they could. One guy had more than a little first aid training and quickly decided the wound was bad enough that Duke needed professional care. Rather than call an ambulance they put Duke in the back of a jeep they had near for that very reason and hauled him off to a local medical center. One of the lifeguards let me know the address. Gabe took control of Duke's board and we headed to the Buggy to get to the treatment center as fast as we could.

At the little clinic, an attendant at the front told us Duke was in something called triage. I had no idea what that meant but it sounded serious. Little did I know it only meant they were checking him out. Why can't people just speak English?

After what seemed like hours, a nurse came out pushing Duke in a wheelchair. He had a large bandage on this forehead and his trunks were caked with blood, but he was clearly alive.

"Oh no, dude, can't you walk?" Gabe asked, genuinely freaked out.

"No, man, they just wouldn't let me," Duke said, rolling his eyes.

I looked at the nurse and asked what was up.

"Your buddy has a nasty gash on his forehead. The cut did require a few stitches. He also probably has a concussion, but he should be okay after resting a few days.", she noted, "He needs to take it easy and check back with us in a week or so."

"We were planning on traveling on down to Florida," I said.

"This one told us that, but the doctor recommends against it. We need to be sure he doesn't develop bad headaches or any other symptoms. He needs rest.", she instructed.

"Got it," I said.

"I've got a headache now," Duke was holding his head in his hand.

Speaking to me rather than Duke, the nurse said the doctor had given the patient a pain killer and that we could expect him to get a bit drowsy in short order. I was kind of glad to hear that. He would be easier to keep down.

Duke looked miserable and a bit embarrassed but finally became resigned to just sitting on the beach for a few days. I'm sure he was thinking, *Dang, where's Abby when I need a little mothering?* Or maybe not.

We were getting a little low on funds but were able to find a second-rate motel three blocks from the beach. The room wasn't much but it seemed clean. Not having Skipper or a girl with us our standards dropped a bit anyway. The place would do for a few days.

Each morning we would change Duke's bandages, have breakfast and head for the beach. Duke continued to fight the idea that he really couldn't surf until they checked him out, but at least he didn't develop any more headaches. I did have a great time surfing near the pier and Gabe seemed to be really enjoying photographing my better rides. We would definitely have to start developing them when we got to Florida and could replenish our cash supply.

After about a week, the day came that the clinic suggested we head back over for them to look at Duke's wound and have him tell them how many fingers they were holding up. Duke disappeared back into the treatment rooms and after a while came walking back out. That was a good sign. They didn't use a wheelchair.

"It's cool," Duke said. "I'm good to go."

The nurse came out behind him and gave me the thumbs up. I was glad she did because I wasn't at all sure I would have believed Duke.

After we left the clinic Duke laughed and said, "Man they always hold up three fingers." Not sure he was right about that but were very happy he got the all clear.

We headed back to the motel, grabbed our boards and went back over to the pier for a few more rides before moving on. It was clear Duke was a little spooked from his wipeout and picked some fairly wimpy waves to ride. I couldn't blame him. Gabe said it was the worst wipeout he could recall seeing. In thinking about it, I was really glad Abby hadn't seen it.

During our travels, we quickly found out that almost every surfer we ran into had a recommendation for where to go to find the best east coast breaks. Same thing happened in Nags Head. While Duke was recovering, he had time to strike up some conversations on the beach with local guys. At least two told him that something really exciting seemed to be going on down in Wrightsville Beach. I hadn't even heard of that beach but I had heard of Wilmington, a town just a few miles from the oceanfront.

Since Wrightsville was more or less on our way, we decided to head on over and find out what everyone was talking about. It didn't take long to drive down the coast to our next destination. When we got there, we followed our normal routine and began asking around about the best waves. During that search we learned about the Wrightsville Beach Surf Club. I was pretty amazed at all the clubs on the East Coast. We met a few of the guys and found them friendly and happy to help us try out their little corner of paradise.

I even met a guy named Skipper who told me that we'd missed their big event of the year. (*Where in the world did all these Skippers and Skips come from*) I thought. The competition was called the Spring Surf Festival and happened, well, each spring. He said it was a major event for the area and press coverage was heavy. The prior year Greg Noll had even shown up. He didn't compete but caused quite a stir just by being there. Greg as one of my heroes. They called him 'Da Bull' because of his stocky build and aggressive style of addressing the wave. Greg was a big wave surfer and known in California and Hawaii as fearless. I was really disappointed to have missed him the year before but thought maybe I could catch with him and shake his hand at some point. You can only hope.

As we surveyed the beach, I was pretty impressed with the break at something called the Lumina Pavilion. I could tell this huge old structure had likely once been the center of the action on Wrightsville Beach. Skipper had taken us over and told us it had been a dance hall, beach club and even had been a bowling alley. He added that the locals hated to see the place run down. I got a kick out of telling Skipper (the guy not the pup) that we named our dog after him. He wasn't buying it, of course but laughed along anyway. We joined some other folks getting ready to head into the water. Interestingly, a fair number of guys came down from Virginia Beach. I guess Wrightsville had earned its reputation.

Skipper had to shove off, so we told him we really appreciated the welcome and suggestions. Time to head back into the surf. It seemed like Duke had regained his confidence and as we paddled out, he was clearly stoked about getting back into some real surfing. It was a bright, sunny day and at the waters edge you could see for miles and miles up and down the beach.

The air was thick with sea spray. I wasn't aware of any weather off the coast, but the waves were big enough to make you think there was a hurricane somewhere out there. Of course, we loved it and took full advantage.

Gabe continued to take pictures and seemed to be getting more enthusiastic about his new role as team photographer. He also continued to ask around about a competition but by this time of the year most had already happened. That reminded us that we really did have to find other means of funding our activities and just settled in for a couple of days of surfing. Since we were down to just the guys, we decided to sleep in the Buggy for a few hours rather than spend the money for a motel. That turned out to be a bad decision.

We settled down to sleep at about eleven PM that night thinking we would get in some morning surfing then think about moving on. At about midnight, we heard someone tapping on the driver's side window. I immediately thought it was a cop telling us to move along so I rolled down my window only to be face to face with a big mean looking dude who clearly intended no good. His clothes were dirty and his hair matted. I could smell days of bad hygiene immediately.

"I need your money right now!" he demanded in almost a yell. He looked into the car and even though he was alone, must have figured us for a group of hippie surfers who wouldn't put up a fight.

"No, man, we don't have anything for you," I retorted, trying to roll up the window.

The guy reached in and grabbed me by the hair, banging my head forward against the steering wheel. I immediately saw stars. That's when Gabe jumped out of the back seat and just clocked the guy, who crumpled to the ground in a heap. Gabe hit him so hard I almost felt sorry for him. Well almost.

Gabe stood over him his fist still clenched, as if he expected the guy to get up and fight back, but it was clear he was out cold. We all got out of the car and tried to determine if we should call the police.

"I don't think it's worth it," Duke said, "I think this guy is just a bum or a junky or something. Probably didn't even realize what he was doing."

After satisfying ourselves that the guy was still breathing, we decided to move on down the beach a bit and try to get a little more sleep. I knew I would wake up with a headache but was just glad the dude didn't have a gun.

"Wow, Gabe, you are one bad man," Duke said, laughing as we drove off.

Gabe looked almost embarrassed but said, "I don't like anybody messing with my friends."

Clearly.

While our final several hours in Wrightsville Beach were a little more challenging than the first day, we did enjoy a morning of surfing before heading out. Duke was back to his old form and caught the best wave of the day. I was happy to see it and happy to be with my pals as we got ready to move on.

We decided to head directly back to Daytona and Duke was superf happy with that decision. I was really glad that Duke had regained his confidence before he got back to his home beach. So, we headed on to Daytona, deciding not to make any more side trips. After all, I had to see Andy about getting my job back.

Chapter Thirteen

LAZY FLORIDA DAYS (NOT SO MUCH)

When we got to Daytona, we immediately headed over to Jack's. Andy came bounding out and grabbed me in a bear hug that took my breath away.

"I told you we would be back," I said. "In fact, we haven't really been gone that long you know."

"Yep and I knew you were coming.", Andy smiled broadly.

"Huh?"

"We got a letter from Abby. It was addressed to the 'Daytona gang' care of the shop," Andy explained.

"Well what did she say?" I asked, completely surprised that her letter beat us back to Daytona.

Andy handed me the letter and I was relieved to read what she wrote. Turns out she got a ride from Virginia all the way to Providence, Rhode Island and was able to hitchhike over to New Bedford quickly from there. No hassles, no creeps. She was really fortunate, but boy were we very happy she had reached home turf.

She explained that she had a second cousin still living there that would put her up for a few days until she could get a job and a place of her own, at least for the fall. I wondered out loud why anyone would want to spend any cold weather time in coastal Massachusetts, but to each his or her own, I guess. Hopefully as the temperature dropped so would her resolve.

Abby ended the rather lengthy letter saying, *love all you guys*. I'm not sure I'd ever heard her say the word 'love', but it was clear to me that we all loved her and wanted her to rejoin us by the holidays.

Andy had no problem rehiring me and Gabe also got a shift. Duke laid low for a few days until he could figure out what he wanted to do. I was glad to be bringing in a regular pay check and working at a surf shop, it was pretty easy to get the owner to understand the need to head over to the water when the surf was up. But I didn't take advantage of that and worked pretty hard to boost sales.

Since I'd won over at Sebastian Inlet, my reputation had grown a little more out of proportion to my actual accomplishments, but neither Andy or I wanted to burst that bubble.

I was kind of surprised, but Duke ended up going back to the furniture store telling his dad he would stay until the Christmas rush was over. He later told me he wanted to carry his own weight with the team.

After a month and a half in Daytona, two very attractive girls walked into the shop. Alexa and Stacy! They actually showed up! I was stunned but very happy to see them. After hugs, getting reacquainted and introducing Andy, we all agreed to meet for dinner and talk about more comfortable living arrangements. Gabe and I had been crashing with Andy and Duke went back to Ormond Beach and his parent's place. Again, he was miserable but the thought of all of us renting a house perked him up considerably.

It took a couple of weeks before we could find anyone who would rent to us. We pretty quickly learned to let the girls do the talking. After all, they could dress nice and convince the landlords they were just a couple of clean-cut college kids with a couple of equally reliable friends. *Right.*

Finally, we found a big ranch style home in Ormond Beach around a place called Elinor Village that would suit our needs. It was a little stucco rancher that was painted an almost pale pink color. It looked exactly like all the other houses on the street except that each had what Stacy called different "ice cream colors".

We all moved in and staked out our rooms and discussed rules that we would all need to follow. First of all, the girls needed their privacy. They had first dibs on bathroom access. We had two full baths, so it didn't present much of a problem, but it was good that they demanded some respect. We also made sure we could accommodate Abby if she returned.

As summer turned to fall and October began to cool things off just a bit, Andy called me into his little office area behind the shop. We got along great, so I wasn't concerned. Anyway, he was smiling ear to ear.

"You remember me telling you I wanted to design boards for the shop?", Andy reminded me.

"Sure, and you wanted to put the Jack's logo on them.", I responded, thinking it was a great idea.

"I've changed my mind."

"Oh, we aren't going to design our own boards?", I was a little confused at that decision.

"That's not what I mean".

Andy held up a piece of white cardboard with a roughed-out sketch of another logo. It was a dark silhouette of a goofy foot surfer riding on top of a great crest. Below it in really artistic letters it said:

Corkboards

"So, we're going to make boards out of cork? I don't think that would work," I asked, clearly missing the entire point.

"No dude, the guy on the board is supposed to be you. The name comes from your nickname."

I was floored. I didn't know anything about making boards and told Andy so.

"Naw, that's not the way it works. I'm hiring a guy who does make boards and he will make one that you feel comfortable using.", Andy explained. "We'll then start making them to order using the new logo. You'll get your normal commission plus a licensing fee for using your name."

"Say what?"

"What do you think?" Andy asked.

I was silent for a good while but couldn't find a single reason I would object.

"I'm in," I said. And I was.

The entire fall was a whirlwind of activity as we settled into our house, launched the Corkboards brand and did some surfing. I had grown pretty close to Alexa and I guess we'd become a couple. Duke went out with Stacy a couple of times but that didn't seem to be working out the way he might have wanted it. On the other hand, he also talked about Abby a good bit.

By the time Thanksgiving week rolled around, the shop was doing well, and I was learning a lot more about business than I'd ever imagined. I had to understand gross margins, cost of goods sold. It went on and on. My head was spinning. I was glad to have surfing to clear my mind on a daily basis.

I'd become pretty well known around Daytona even to the point of having people I didn't know or couldn't recall meeting walk by me on the street and say, "Hey Corky, how's it going?"

We'd planned a pretty traditional Thanksgiving at the house in Ormond Beach. We invited Andy and his girlfriend Daisy (I kid you not) along with Leslie from the restaurant. We all contributed to the dinner in our own way. As we were waiting for the turkey to finish up and standing around the kitchen talking, the doorbell rang.

Gabe answered it and I heard, "Abby!" coming from the living room. We all rushed in and there were hugs all around.

"I told you I'd catch up with you," Abby said.

"How did you even know where to find us?" I wondered out loud.

"I wanted to surprise you, so I kept in touch with Leslie."

Leslie blushed a bit but loved being part of the surprise, I could tell. Skipper had followed Abby in and Gabe was down on the floor welcoming him back with ear scratching and offering his cheek for dog kissing. Even Skipper seemed to understand how happy we all were to be together again.

After more hugs and kisses, we showed Abby where she could freshen up. Stacy checked on the turkey and declared it ready to serve, so we all brought our dishes to the table and sat down for Thanksgiving, Florida style. Abby pointed out that where she had been a week or so earlier it was forty-five degrees. In Daytona is was near eighty. No contest.

Against Andy's advice, given the huge meal, Duke and I headed to the beach to catch a wave or two. During dinner, we learned that Abby would be returning to work for Leslie. So, we were in pretty good financial shape and even able to sock away some funds for future travels, even though we all knew that if the team hit the road again Andy wouldn't likely be quite so forgiving. We would have to cross that bridge when we came to it.

When Gabe had built up a little extra cash, he started getting some of his pictures developed. We were all really impressed with what we saw.

"Gabe, you're an artist with a camera," Abby said, "I'm serious."

We all had to agree. Gabe was somewhat more critical of his work, but he had to be proud. I thought that just maybe he had found his lifelong work.

Before the year ended there was still surfing to do and Duke and I were determined to surf every day, come hell or high water (well, I mean, high water was actually a good thing!)

Surfing in November could be good or bad depending to the tail end of hurricane season. Even a tropical storm could churn up some pretty good surf if it was anywhere near the coast. I guess we were lucky. It was pretty late in the hurricane season but there was tropical weather headed our way and we were determined to take advantage. The guy on the television said the storm wouldn't hit us head on but stay about twenty miles off the coast and work its way up to make landfall somewhere in North Carolina, presuming there was anything left of it.

It was supposed to have the greatest impact on the Florida coast on the Saturday following Thanksgiving. We woke up that day full of anticipation. Alexa and Stacy decided to join us in catching what we hoped would be some really fine waves. Gabe packed up his camera and headed out with us to take some shots and I noticed Abby had her ratty old three ring binder. She told me she had had it with her since high school and you could certainly tell it was well used.

When we got to the beach the sky looked pretty threatening. If I had to guess I would have figured the storm was closer than twenty miles. But, hey, I'm no weatherman.

Duke, Alexa, Stacy and I all paddled out together and sat waiting for a really good ride. Finally, we saw a monster of a wave forming. We looked at each other, laughed and started to paddle into it. Mike, another California surfing buddy of mine, once described a particular break as *"Overhead sets super consistent corduroy as far as the eye could see, not a drop of water out of place."* I think Mike was just as much a poet as surfer. It fit the day perfectly.

We were all able to get up and were riding virtually side by side for quite a while. I was really surprised that we all rode that wave all the way in.

Gabe came running up to us before we could paddle back out.

"Damn, you won't believe the photographs I got. I hope they come out." He was almost giddy.

We caught a couple more nice waves, but started getting a little concerned as the wind picked up.

"Maybe we should head back to the house," Stacy suggested. She had experienced a hurricane first hand and let us know this didn't look all that different. She said riding out the storm had been the scariest night of her life. She wasn't keen on reliving that experience but knew that we didn't want to get caught on the beach, so we took her advice.

Sure enough, the weatherman had been wrong, and the storm took a hard left hand turn and plowed right into the Daytona Beach area. It wasn't declared a hurricane but later they said it was a pretty strong tropical storm. It was enough for us as the house rattled and wind driven rain was getting in everywhere.

The storm didn't last that long but left us all a little spooked. I worried about how Skipper would react, but he seemed to be the calmest houseguest of all. Good boy!

Soon the hurricane season was *really* over, and we began to see the signs of Christmas. While it wasn't peak tourist season, the snowbirds had come to town looking for better weather and the shop had gotten really busy. Seemed like everyone was giving a surfing related gift or at least a souvenir t-shirt. One of our best sellers turned out to be one with the Corkboards logo on it and I got a little royalty on each one of those in addition to the boards. I couldn't believe I had lucked into this situation.

As for gifts for each other, we drew names and agreed to a limit and that funny gifts were the best bet. We decided to swap gifts on Christmas morning, since most of us grew up that way. I had to admit that I looked forward to getting up that special day surrounded by people who had become good friends. My mom always told me Christmas was about spending time with the ones you love, and I thought this qualified. It was enough to make a surfer cry. Well maybe not but when we got up, I was in a great mood and looking forward to the day.

The gifts were about as goofy as you could get. Stacy had become sort of the house mother. Gabe drew her name and bought her a set of potholders with palm trees and flamingos. Duke drew Alexa and found her a little bracelet that said *girl surfer*. Not *surfer girl* but *girl surfer*. I wish I'd found that.

The rest of the gifts were of that type and when we were finished with our little swap, Gabe said he had 'gone off script, as he called it and had an extra gift for each of us. He had a way with words. The 'gift of Gabe' at its best.

Behind the couch he'd hidden five wrapped packages. He may have had a way with words but wrapping Christmas gifts wasn't one of his skills. No matter, he handed one to each of us. They were all the same size and square. It was about the size of a record album but thicker and heavier.

Duke guessed it was a boxed set of Beachboys records. Alexa joked that it was probably a set of steak knives.

Gabe asked us to wait and open the packages together so that he could get a picture. Once he was set, he told us to go ahead and peel off the paper. I think we were all really surprised by what we found inside. They perfectly framed photos of four surfers riding an awesome break side by side, two girls and two guys. Each seemed to have perfect style and all of the surfers seemed to be smiling.

It took a minute before we realized it was me, Duke, Alexa and Stacy surfing the storm the Saturday after Thanksgiving. It came back to me how excited Gabe had been after that ride. He'd caught the image at exactly the right moment. I knew then that my buddy was a man of real vision. I imagined that he might end up being someone who would keep a pictorial record of great moments in surfing.

Turns out I was right.

Just for laughs, I made a mental note that we never made it to Milwaukee that trip. Maybe next year.

Chapter Fourteen

TRANSITION

It was a heck of a story. I just had to paint it.
    Abby Colter-Phillips.

Chapter Fifteen

THE PITCH

So, like I said before, my name is Corky Sandoval. At least it is now. Or at least that's what people think. That is, most people.

I know, you're confused. Sometimes so am I. So maybe we should start at the *actual* beginning.

I was born Gregory Priestly. I was told by my parents that our last name meant 'of the church' or something like that. I wasn't then and I'm not now, but that has nothing to do with our story.

I grew up in a small town in Ohio in a house by a river. My dad was a steelworker and my mom a homemaker. Even those facts have little to do with our story, but it gives you some perspective.

It was during my junior year of high school that I realized I had to get out of that river town and just go **DO** something. I wasn't certain what I should do, mind you, but I knew it wasn't going to get done in that little town and I was pretty sure not in the great state of Ohio. Luckily, I figured out that I would need some sort of education if I was going to determine the course my life would take. So, I managed to keep my grades up to the point that I had multiple choices when considering colleges. By the time my class graduated, most of my friends had committed to Ohio State, Ohio University or University of Cincinnati. Good choices all but suffice it to say that I only applied to out of state schools.

I focused my attention on schools in Florida and California at first. After all there was all that good weather and the promise of meeting those 'girls on the beach' that the Beachboys song made famous. But then my friend Glen convinced me to take a look at the schools in Virginia (after all they have a beach there) and I ended up attending the University of Virginia on a grant in aid. I must say I didn't hate my four years there. Notice I didn't say I loved it. I mean I loved certain aspects about college life. The football and basketball games (although while I was there our teams were not stellar), frat parties and casual dating. Even some of the classes were stimulating but it took me nearly halfway through my second year before I had any clue what I wanted to do professionally.

I'd put my nose to the old grindstone and ended up with a business degree with emphasis on accounting. Yep accounting. Didn't see that one coming, did you? Neither did I. But in my junior and senior years at UVA, I began to see that what they then called 'data processing' was going to fundamentally change the way people did business. I worked hard to keep my grades up but found myself spending a great deal of time in the computer center fiddling with the card punches, remote terminals and clunky printers. So, by the time I hit the job market, I was a bit ahead of the other would-be accountants in that I actually understood something about what made computers tick.

Eventually, I was offered a job with one of the 'Big Six' accounting firms at the Chicago office. After all, they were impressed with that kid with a shiny new degree from Mr. Jefferson's university and a working knowledge of computing.

I suppose I was ambitious. At least ambitious enough to work my way up the organization step by step. Before I knew it twenty years had passed, and I was on the verge of making partner.

By then, I had met and married a great young lady from Boston named Lisa-Michelle Longfield, a petite vivacious brunette with ambitions of her own. Lee, as I call her, had wanted to be an artist but faced with the reality of making little money in fine arts opted to study graphic design. When we met, she was working with an advertising agency and doing quite well. Between us we enjoyed a very comfortable lifestyle with a downtown condo, a two year old Mercedes and a Jack Russell named Shecky (I honestly can't recall why).

I think that being offered the partnership was my first critical juncture in an otherwise work a day life and one that would begin to define my future and largely that of my little family. I just wasn't inclined to accept the partnership and let Lee know my feelings. To say she was surprised would be an understatement. I know she had serious misgivings, but I painted a picture of a bit more independence and described the smell of salty ocean breezes.

At this point you may think we moved back to Laguna, but you have to remember that was part of the first part of this story. Try to keep things straight, will you?

So, with Lee beginning to understand how my dream had evolved, I turned down the partnership, resigned, sold the condo, packed up our Mercedes and a trailer and moved to Virginia Beach where I opened my own practice. Based upon her credentials, Lisa-Michelle was able to join a reputable ad agency in Norfolk and our life took off.

Since we have some equity cash from selling the condo in Chicago, we were able to buy a small house a block from the beach. We came to love that little house and enjoyed the beach every day, even as my practice struggled to take root. Finally, I had built up a fairly reliable group of clients and Chicago once and for all faded into the rearview mirror.

Another twenty years went by pretty quickly, it seemed. We had decided not to have kids but had a succession of Jack Russell's after losing Shecky to a lung problem shortly after the move.

After twenty years of enjoying the Virginia lifestyle I had come to another critical juncture. I know you have already anticipated that I got that itch again to move on. As much as I enjoyed our life in Virginia, I felt as though my little accounting practice had evolved into a mini-Big Six firm (although by then I think there are only four).

So, I decided I had to find the time to ask Lee one simple question. I waited until we were sitting on our small patio enjoying a late day drink and reading the Virginian Pilot. She always spent time reading the business news while I hungrily consumed the sports page.

"What's next?" I asked.

"Um, what do you mean, Greg?" she asked, at first not looking up from the paper. Then she peered over the edge with a quizzical look on her face. "What's on your mind, Greg?"

Not wanting to totally scare the bejesus out of her, I proceeded cautiously.

"Well, we've been here for twenty years and I sure would like to talk about a change of scenery," I said, venturing carefully.

"You mean you'd like to move to Newport News or maybe Norfolk?" Lee asked. "The real estate market is pretty good right now, so we can probably afford a bigger home in one of the nicer neighborhoods."

"Um…not exactly what I had in mind. I've been doing accounting for most of my life and I guess for many of those years I've had a completely different dream," I said still cautiously, watching the look on her face change.

"Come on, Greg, why haven't you mentioned this before?"

"Because I thought it would seem frivolous and unrealistic."

"You might as well tell me what you have in mind. I need to know so that I can formulate an appropriate counterpoint," Lee said, rather appropriately. "You want to be a pirate or a dog trainer or maybe an astronaut?"

I could tell by her tone that she was trying to be funny, but the conversation was starting to make me a little uncomfortable. None-the-less, I ventured on.

"Lee, have you ever fantasized about being a completely different person with a different past and totally different goals?"

Lee was getting confused at this point.

"What's wrong with Greg Priestly? After all that's the man I married, and he seems like a pretty good guy. And I thought he was happy."

"I am happy, Lee. At least mostly."

I couldn't tell if Lee as simply concerned or getting annoyed.

"Is it me, Greg?"

"Oh no Lisa-Michelle! I should have told you right up front that you are the one aspect of my life I'm truly happy with."

"You never call me Lisa-Michelle any more unless there is bad news. Did you sell the business or rob a bank or something?"

As if those two possibilities were equally distasteful.

"Of course not. Anyway, I wouldn't make any life changing decision without talking with you."

"Then what?"

Okay here goes.

"Alright then, since I was a teenager I think I've had this alter ego. It started when my folks almost moved to Florida. My dad's dream was always to live there, enjoy the great weather and pursue his dream of opening a convenience store or neighborhood bar or something. I never understood why other than how tough it was working in a steel mill."

"Okay," Lee said. "Let's get to your fantasy."

"Well, my folks used to take us to Florida once a year on vacation and I began to notice the teenaged boys on the beach with their huge surfboards. They all seemed to be perfectly tanned and physically fit. Getting to know some of them during vacation of course, many were one can short of a six pack, but that's neither here nor there."

"Uh-huh."

"But over time I'd fall asleep dreaming about learning to surf, growing my hair and basically hanging out at the beach. Of course, making a living never crossed my mind, but the fantasy was vivid. I even made up a name for myself."

"Puddinhead?" Lee chuckled but was clearly mocking me.

"I tried out several combinations of names that sounded like a surfer and finally landed on Corky Sandoval."

"You're not Hispanic. Isn't Sandoval Hispanic?"

"You're right but that's beside the point. I was inventing a whole new me. I even made up stories about moving from the West Coast after having lived the life of a surf bum. I must have reworked and tweaked Corky's background forty or fifty times and eventually he seemed very real to me. So, in that sense, I am Corky to some degree. See what I mean?"

"Nope."

We sat there for a moment and I saw a look of confusion on Lee's face. I could sense she was getting agitated, more so than I anticipated. I think she thought our entire life was in question. I really didn't want to hurt her but thought she should know about my little fantasy. I thought it was harmless. Clearly, she didn't agree.

"Time out."

Lisa-Michelle always used those two words to indicate that the conversation was over, at least for the moment. It usually meant that she was either steamed with me and didn't want to say something she would later regret, or she was confused. I think this might have been a combination of both.

I clammed up and we went on with our evening.

The next morning, I woke up with the radio alarm playing *Wouldn't It Be Nice* of all things. Of course, it had to be the Beachboys. I love the Beachboys but this particular morning it just pointed out that I hadn't made much headway the prior evening.

I have to say I was really surprised when Lee brought up the discussion at breakfast.

"So, what's the bottom line on your Corky fantasy, Greg?", Lee asked over eggs-benedict.

"Are you sure you want to know?"

"Well, you took it this far and it seems to mean a lot to you, so shoot."

I began laying out a vision of liquidating our worldly goods, moving to a more tropical location and beginning again. For several years, and like many men, I had wanted to open my own bar and grill. As my vision for a beachfront tiki bar evolved, so did the fantasy of a new life as Corky. Eventually I imagined owning Corky's, a bar with a surfing theme. I would assume the persona of Corky and base the surroundings on his legacy of winning surf competitions back in the day.

"You mean to say you would give up everything about our life now to *become* this surfer character? What about our families and friends? Would we be able to earn a living running a bar?" Lee asked.

I had to admit I hadn't thought the idea through completely and didn't have immediate answers.

"I think if we put our heads together we could make a go of it.", said in my best sales mode, "I mean, I'm an accountant and your business is about promoting things. Surely, we're smart enough to pull it off."

"Would it mean I have to give up my identity and play some sort of character?".

"Not necessarily, but it could be fun for you too. You could be an ex-hooker with a heart of gold," I said facetiously.

"No, no, no!"

"I was only kidding, Lee, but you could spin a little background for yourself that filled in some of the blanks in Corky's story."

"What if someone outed you? Maybe someone from the old firm or one of your current clients?"

"Well, we would just have to cross that bridge when we come to it, or as Buffet said, "*burn that bridge when we come to it,*" I said, chuckling.

I could tell no amount of levity was getting through.

"Look, Lee, just do me a favor and sleep on it. I'm ready for a new adventure but if you decide you aren't, we'll just forget it."

Lisa-Michelle had a blank look on her face but finally said, "I guess I owe you that much. Let's talk again tomorrow. I can't get my head around it right now, but I'll think it through."

I kissed her on the cheek, not venturing a real kiss and she flinched just a bit. Not a good sign.

"Thanks, honey," I said, settling for a small win.

That night I lay awake for several hours just going over the plans for the bar. In my mind, I knew exactly the type of beachfront community I envisioned settling in, what the property would look like and even the type food we would serve. Of course, it had to have a surfing theme and I thought maybe I would decorate with black and white pictures of famous surfers riding big waves. I wanted indoor and outdoor seating. Behind the bar I decided a big screen tv showing surf competitions would work since I hoped my clientele would enjoy the work of real artists with the board.

I was a fan of a Virginia Beach based food boat called The Barnacle. At one point I had toyed with the idea of having my bar on a boat but realized pretty quickly that I knew nothing about boating and that the boat would have to be huge.

One thing I knew with certainty was the type of music I'd have on the jukebox. Oh yeah, a jukebox with real records. No piped in music for me. In my mind I heard the Ventures, the Surfaris, Dick Dale and the Deltones and even the Beachboys and Jan and Dean. I knew the last two weren't as legit as the early surf music stars, but most people held them out to be leaders of the surf and hot rod era music era. Yep, you had to cater to your clientele. And I had a pretty good idea of who would be attracted to the little oasis. Snowbirds who longed to live the beach bum life, actual surfers who needed a place of their own, college kids on spring break into the whole nostalgia thing. Yep those were the logical targets.

Maybe I'd even have a little gift shop with souvenir t-shirts, surf music CD's, books on surfing, that sort of thing. Of course, I'd have to be careful about the books. Wouldn't want the clientele to become experts at surfing history and who won what. They just had to buy into the vision, the romance and enjoy the vibe. With some help

I could make it all happen, I knew I could. I lay awake smiling at the thought.

Up until that sleepless night I hadn't put much thought into a name for the place. I started running ideas through my head. Sandovals, Surfin' Bird, Big Waves, Corktop's. I really didn't like any of them. Finally, I settled on *Corky's Beach Bar.* Just had a nice ring to it. And the logo would be the silhouette of a lone surfer, on the crest of a big wave above the name Corky's. Below that in smaller letters would be the Beach Bar part. But that design could wait for another day. Heck, Lee could even help me design it. Yep…that's the ticket.

I wanted to take my time and hire the very best waitstaff, bartenders and cooks I could afford. In the front of the house I wanted big smiles, great attitudes and good humor. I decided that waiters and waitresses and particularly bartenders needed to be performers in their own way. In the back of the house I wanted a head cook who took our bar food to the next level.

In the end, all of this turned on the decision Lee had to make. Was she with me or not? I really didn't know what to expect. What I did know was that I had a couple of accounting clients coming in the next day and forced myself to reign in the fantasizing. It was difficult, but I finally fell asleep.

Unfortunately, I had a pretty bad dream that the whole idea had become a big mess and that Lisa-Michelle had left me for a more stable life. I woke up sweating and hoping I knew what I was doing in bringing her this idea. I had no clue what to expect from her. I would find out soon.

Chapter Sixteen

TO BE OR NOT TO BE

As I said, the next day was a 'school day', as we used to kid, so both Lee and I needed to head off to work as normal. Before we kissed goodbye and wished each other a good day, Lee suggested we meet at an ocean front bar called Mahi Mahs for a cocktail after work. I readily accepted, in part because I knew she wouldn't be too hard on me in public.

When I walked in at five-thirty, Lee was already there and had ordered our usual drinks. With me, it was a Bombay Sapphire and tonic and she preferred a dirty vodka martini, Grey Goose if you please. That was a good sign as was the normal warm smile she had on her face when we reunited after work. I was growing hopeful.

"Well, Lee, have you done some more thinking about our discussion?"

Taking a sip of her martini Lee looked at me and paused just a bit too long in my mind. I braced for a wholesale rejection.

"Here's the way I feel," Lee began, "We've had a hell of a ride so far and there are only so many years left."

"Jeez, Lee, I hope there are twenty or more," I said.

"Beside the point for this discussion. I'm not being morbid, just realistic. Anyway, hear me out, will you?"

"Sorry."

"I think it is more than a little weird. I also think it could mean we lose everything we've worked so hard for."

My heart sank.

"With that said I agree that a new adventure is appealing to me too, but with certain stipulations."

"I'm listening." Using my Frasier Crane voice.

"First, if I'm going to be part of building these new personas and the business, I want a say in every major decision."

"Of course." No hesitation on my part. I always thought she had a sharper business mind than mine anyway.

"Second, we have to run the place like a real business. I mean things like no free drinks for the boys."

"What boys?"

Lee looked at me with a little disdain. "You're missing my point. You know as well as I do that there *will* be boys. Hangers on, frequent flyers. I'm sure you know what I mean, right?"

"Right. Anything else?"

"Yes, I want you to promise if you're busted you're busted. If someone figures out you are really Greg Priestly or that Corky what's his name is just a character, you won't lie about it. I mean you can explain it away as a marketing gimmick or something, but I just don't want to be part of a huge lie and have to remember all the details all the time. Too much stress and leaving stress behind is part of the goal isn't it?"

"It is. Might be the most important part in fact."

"So, do we have a deal?" Lee asked, holding out her hand.

I shook her hand like I might have a client rather than my wife and said, "Deal!"

And so, began the task of taking apart one life and beginning another one. I had no idea what a big job it would be. I would soon find out.

And the legend continues…..

The End (for now)

Coming Attractions

Here's an excerpt from Phil Perkins' next book *"Corky's Beach Bar"* **due out soon.**

One Saturday afternoon in May, Lee was stuck at her office working on an upcoming pitch to a potentially large client in Richmond. I decided to head for the beach anyway and was naturally drawn to the surfing area. Most of the surfers were quite young, although there was an occasional geezer out there unwilling or unable to give up the sport he loved and thereby give in to advancing age. I had to admit I totally got it. Reminded me of a song called "I Will Not Go Quietly".

I decided to approach one of the older surfers to find out a bit more about what motivated him. As I approached him on the beach I tried to find a way to introduce myself in a way that didn't present me as some sort of surf groupie, but pretty much failed.

"Excuse, me, I couldn't help but notice you caught some fairly good waves out there. Must be kind of challenging", I blurted out sounding every bit as nerdy as I felt.

"Nah, if you pay attention to what the ocean is telling you, you can find a way to catch a ride."

"I'm sorry, I'm Greg, Greg Priestly", I said sticking out my hand, "I guess I'm just a would-be surfer at heart", I admitted.

"I'm Joey Richfield. Folks call me JR", he responded completing the handshake.

"I didn't mean to interrupt your day, JR", I said, "If you're busy I understand."

"It's cool. I was about to take a break anyway. Are you a tourist or what?"

Sizing JR up I figured him to be in his 50s. He had one of those enviable tans everyone wanted before they figured out how bad tanning was for your skin. He was extremely fit, I assumed because of surfing, and had longish dark hair with streaks of gray.

"Actually, I'm a local", I answered, "I live further on up the beach. I've just grown really interested in surfing lately."

"So, you should try it!"

"Seems like I might be a little old to start now", I said hoping I didn't insult the man, "Watching you I guess you've been surfing since you were a kid."

"Your guess would be way off. I actually only started about 5 years ago. I gave myself my first board on my 50th birthday in fact.", JR responding smiling broadly.

I think JR got a kick out of my assumption that he had great surfing skills.

"Wow…good for you!", could I have sounded any more goofy?

"I was kind of like you, just watching from the beach. When I turned 50 I started to wonder if my proverbial ship had sailed and decided to prove to myself I could still learn new things."

144

Listening to JR talk I quickly realized that this was a professional man. Someone with a white-collar job but who wanted more out of life. I certainly understood that pull.

"And what do you do, Greg?", JR asked.

"Hate to even admit it but I'm an accountant. I have my own firm", I replied.

"Well I can top that as far as hating to admit it. I'm an attorney. Not the fun kind either, just corporate."

We both had a laugh at our own expense. Somehow, I couldn't imagine JR being called 'Joey' at the office. Might be a name he uses on the beach when some schmuck comes up and interrupts his surfing.

"Say JR, do you have time for beer?"

"I'll make time."